Penguin Books

The Book of Sand

Jorge Luis Borges was born in Buenos Aires in 1899 and was educated in Europe. One of the major writers of our time, he has published many collections of poems, essays, and short stories. In 1961, Borges shared the International Publishers' Prize with Samuel Beckett. The Ingram Merrill Foundation granted him its Annual Literary Award in 1966 for his 'outstanding contribution to literature'. In 1970 he was awarded the degree of Doctor of Letters, *honoris causa*, from both Columbia and Oxford, the following year won the fifth biennial Jerusalem Prize, and in 1973 was awarded the Alfonso Reyes Prize. *Time* has called him 'the greatest living writer in the Spanish language today', while the *New York Herald Tribune* has described him as 'unquestionably the most brilliant South American writing today'. He was Director of the National Library of Buenos Aires from 1955 until 1973.

A Universal History of Infamy, *Labyrinths*, *The Book of Imaginary Beings* and *Doctor Brodie's Report* have been published in Penguins.

Norman Thomas di Giovanni, who to date has produced English versions of eight books by Borges, lives in Devon. He worked with Borges in Buenos Aires from 1968 to 1972.

Alastair Reid is a noted poet and translator. He made his selection for *The Gold of the Tigers* from two books of poetry by Borges: *El oro de los tigres* (1972) and *La rosa profunda* (1975).

Jorge Luis Borges

Penguin Books

The Book of Sand

The Book of Sand
Translated by Norman Thomas di Giovanni

The Gold of the Tigers
Selected Later Poems: translated by Alastair Reid

p goodfellow

Penguin Books Ltd, Harmondsworth, Middlesex, England
Penguin Books, 625 Madison Avenue, New York, New York 10022, U.S.A.
Penguin Books Australia Ltd, Ringwood, Victoria, Australia
Penguin Books Canada Ltd, 2801 John Street, Markham, Ontario, Canada L3R 1B4
Penguin Books (N.Z.) Ltd, 182–190 Wairau Road, Auckland 10, New Zealand

El librole arena first published by Emecé Editores, S.A., 1975
This translation first published in the U.S.A. by E. P. Dutton 1977
Published simultaneously in Penguin Books and Allen Lane 1979
Reprinted 1980

Copyright © Emecé Editores, S.A., and Norman Thomas di Giovanni,
1971, 1975, 1976, 1977, 1979

El oro de los tigres and *La rosa profunda*
first published by Emecé Editores, S.A., 1972 1975
This translation, a selection with English translations from *El oro de los tigres*
and *La rosa profunda*, first published in the U.S.A. by E. P. Dutton 1977
Published simultaneously in Penguin Books and Allen Lane 1979
Copyright © Emecé Editores, S.A., 1972 1975
English translation copyright © Alastair Reid, 1976, 1977, 1979
All rights reserved

The following stories from *The Book of Sand* first appeared in these periodicals:

The Antioch Review: 'The Bribe'

The Atlantic Monthly: 'There Are More Things'

The New Yorker: 'The Congress', 'Utopia of a Tired Man', 'The Disk', 'The
Book of Sand', 'The Mirror and the Mask', 'Avelino Arredondo',
'Undr', 'The Night of the Gifts'

The New York Times Magazine: 'The Sect of the Thirty', 'Ulrike'

Playboy: 'The Other'

'The Congress' has also been published in a limited edition by Enitharmon
Press, London, 1974

The following poems from *The Gold of the Tigers* have appeared in these
publications:

The New Yorker: 'The Watcher', 'The Palace', 'Hengist Wants Men, A.D.
449', 'Brunanburh, A.D. 937', 'To the Nightingale', 'Talismans'

The New York Review of Books: 'The Blind Man', 'A Blind Man', 'Browning
Resolves to be a Poet', 'To the German Language'

Translation: 'The Gold of the Tigers', 'The Unending Rose'

American Poetry Review: 'You', 'Inventory', 'I Am', 'My Books'

New Republic: 'Tankas', 'Fifteen Coins', 'Elegy', 'Milonga of Manuel Flores'
'I', 'Poem of Quantity', 'Susana Bombal'

Made and printed in Great Britain
by Richard Clay (The Chaucer Press) Ltd, Bungay, Suffolk
Set in Monotype Ehrhardt

Contents

The Book of Sand

Translated by Norman Thomas di Giovanni

Author's note

At my age (I was born in 1899), I cannot promise – I
cannot even promise myself – more than these few variations on favourite themes. As everyone knows, this is the
classic recourse of irreparable monotony. Allow me,
nevertheless, to point out one or two details.

The volume includes thirteen stories. The number is
accidental, or fatal – here the two words are strictly
synonymous – and not magical. If of all my stories I had
to save one, I would probably save 'The Congress', which
at the same time is the most autobiographical (the one
richest in memories) and the most imaginative. Nor shall
I hide a predilection for 'The Book of Sand'. There is
also a love story, a 'psychological' story, and the story
of a dramatic episode in South American history.

In these blind man's exercises, I have tried to be faithful
to the example of H. G. Wells in combining a plain and
at times almost colloquial style with a fantastic plot. To
Wells' name the reader may add those of Swift and of Poe,
who, around 1838, gave up a very rich style in order to
bequeath us the admirable final chapters of his *Narrative
of Arthur Gordon Pym*.

I do not write for a select minority, which means nothing
to me, nor for that adulated platonic entity known as
'The Masses'. Both abstractions, so dear to the demago-
gue, I disbelieve in. I write for myself and for my friends,
and I write to ease the passing of time.

The other

It was in Cambridge, back in February, 1969, that the event took place. I made no attempt to record it at the time, because, fearing for my mind, my initial aim was to forget it. Now, some years later, I feel that if I commit it to paper others will read it as a story and, I hope, one day it will become a story for me as well. I know it was horrifying while it lasted – and even more so during the sleepless nights that followed – but this does not mean that an account of it will necessarily move anyone else.

It was about ten o'clock in the morning. I sat on a bench facing the Charles River. Some five hundred yards distant, on my right, rose a tall building whose name I never knew. Ice floes were borne along on the grey water. Inevitably, the river made me think about time – Heraclitus' millennial image. I had slept well; my class on the previous afternoon had, I thought, managed to hold the interest of my students. Not a soul was in sight.

All at once, I had the impression (according to psychologists, it corresponds to a state of fatigue) of having lived that moment once before. Someone had sat down at the other end of the bench. I would have preferred to be alone, but not wishing to appear unsociable I avoided getting up abruptly. The other man had begun to whistle. It was then that the first of the many disquieting things of that morning occurred. What he whistled, what he tried to whistle (I have no ear for music), was the tune of

3

'La tapera', an old milonga by Elías Regules. The melody took me back to a certain Buenos Aires patio, which has long since disappeared, and to the memory of my cousin Álvaro Melián Lafinur, who has been dead for so many years. Then came the words. They were those of the opening line. It was not Álvaro's voice but an imitation of it. Recognizing this, I was taken aback.

'Sir,' I said, turning to the other man, 'are you an Uruguayan or an Argentine?'

'Argentine, but I've lived in Geneva since 1914,' he replied.

There was a long silence. 'At number seventeen Malagnou – across from the Orthodox church?' I asked.

He answered in the affirmative.

'In that case,' I said straight out, 'your name is Jorge Luis Borges. I, too, am Jorge Luis Borges. This is 1969 and we're in the city of Cambridge.'

'No,' he said in a voice that was mine but a bit removed. He paused, then became insistent. 'I'm here in Geneva, on a bench, a few steps from the Rhone. The strange thing is that we resemble each other, but you're much older and your hair is grey.'

'I can prove I'm not lying,' I said. 'I'm going to tell you things a stranger couldn't possibly know. At home we have a silver maté cup with a base in the form of entwined serpents. Our great-grandfather brought it from Peru. There's also a silver washbasin that hung from his saddle. In the wardrobe of your room are two rows of books: the three volumes of Lane's Thousand and One Nights, with steel engravings and with notes in small type at the end of each chapter; Quicherat's Latin dictionary; Tacitus' *Germania* in Latin and also in Gordon's English translation; a *Don Quixote* published by Garnier; Rivera Indarte's *Tablas de Sangre*, inscribed by the author; Carlyle's *Sartor Resartus*; a biography of Amiel; and, hidden behind the other volumes, a book in paper covers

4

about sexual customs in the Balkans. Nor have I forgotten one evening on a certain second floor of the Place Dubourg.'

'Dufour,' he corrected.

'Very well – Dufour. Is this enough now?'

'No,' he said. 'These proofs prove nothing. If I am dreaming you, it's natural that you know what I know. Your catalogue, for all its length, is completely worthless.'

His objection was to the point. I said, 'If this morning and this meeting are dreams, each of us has to believe that he is the dreamer. Perhaps we have stopped dreaming, perhaps not. Our obvious duty, meanwhile, is to accept the dream just as we accept the world and being born and seeing and breathing.'

'And if the dream should go on?' he said anxiously.

To calm him and to calm myself, I feigned an air of assurance that I certainly did not feel. 'My dream has lasted seventy years now,' I said. 'After all, there isn't a person alive who, on waking, does not find himself with himself. It's what is happening to us now – except that we are two. Don't you want to know something of my past, which is the future awaiting you?'

He assented without a word. I went on, a bit lost. 'Mother is healthy and well in her house on Charcas and Maipú, in Buenos Aires, but Father died some thirty years ago. He died of heart trouble. Hemiplegia finished him; his left hand, placed on his right, was like the hand of a child on a giant's. He died impatient for death but without complaint. Our grandmother had died in the same house. A few days before the end, she called us all together and said, "I'm an old woman who is dying very, very slowly. Don't anyone become upset about such a common, everyday thing." Your sister, Norah, married and has two sons. By the way, how is everyone at home?'

'Quite well. Father makes his same antireligious jokes.

Last night he said that Jesus was like the gauchos, who don't like to commit themselves, and that's why he preached in parables.' He hesitated and then said, 'And you?'

'I don't know the number of books you'll write, but I know they'll be too many. You'll write poems that will give you a pleasure that others won't share and stories of a somewhat fantastic nature. Like your father and so many others of our family, you will teach.'

It pleased me that he did not ask about the success or failure of his books. I changed my tone and went on. 'As for history, there was another war, almost among the same antagonists. France was not long in caving in; England and America fought against a German dictator named Hitler – the cyclical battle of Waterloo. Around 1946, Buenos Aires gave birth to another Rosas, who bore a fair resemblance to our kinsman. In 1955, the province of Córdoba came to our rescue, as Entre Ríos had in the last century. Now things are going badly. Russia is taking over the world; America, hampered by the superstition of democracy, can't make up its mind to become an empire. With every day that passes, our country becomes more provincial. More provincial and more pretentious – as if its eyes were closed. It wouldn't surprise me if the teaching of Latin in our schools were replaced by that of Guaraní.'

I could tell that he was barely paying attention. The elemental fear of what is impossible and yet what is so dismayed him. I, who have never been a father, felt for that poor boy – more intimate to me even than a son of my flesh – a surge of love. Seeing that he clutched a book in his hands, I asked what it was.

'*The Possessed*, or, as I believe, *The Devils*, by Fëdor Dostoevski,' he answered, not without vanity.

'It has faded in my memory. What's it like?' As soon as I said this, I felt that the question was a blasphemy.

'The Russian master,' he pronounced, 'has seen better than anyone else into the labyrinth of the Slavic soul.'

This attempt at rhetoric seemed to me proof that he had regained his composure. I asked what other volumes of the master he had read. He mentioned two or three, among them *The Double*. I then asked him if on reading them he could clearly distinguish the characters, as you could in Joseph Conrad, and if he thought of going on in his study of Dostoevski's work.

'Not really,' he said with a certain surprise.

I asked what he was writing and he told me he was putting together a book of poems that would be called *Red Hymns*. He said he had also considered calling it *Red Rhythms*.

'And why not?' I said. 'You can cite good antecedents. Rubén Darío's blue verse and Verlaine's grey song.'

Ignoring this, he explained that his book would celebrate the brotherhood of man. The poet of our time could not turn his back on his own age, he went on to say. I thought for a while and asked if he truly felt himself a brother to everyone – to all funeral directors, for example, to all postmen, to all deep-sea divers, to all those who lived on the even-numbered side of the street, to all those who were aphonic, and so on. He answered that his book referred to the great mass of the oppressed and alienated.

'Your mass of oppressed and alienated is no more than an abstraction,' I said. 'Only individuals exist – if it can be said that anyone exists. "The man of yesterday is not the man of today," some Greek remarked. We two, seated on this bench in Geneva or Cambridge, are perhaps proof of this.'

Except in the strict pages of history, memorable events stand in no need of memorable phrases. At the point of death, a man tries to recall an engraving glimpsed in childhood; about to enter battle, soldiers speak of the mud or of their sergeant. Our situation was unique and,

7

frankly, we were unprepared for it. As fate would have it, we talked about literature; I fear I said no more than the things I usually say to journalists. My alter ego believed in the invention, or discovery, of new metaphors; I, in those metaphors that correspond to intimate and obvious affinities and that our imagination has already accepted. Old age and sunset, dreams and life, the flow of time and water. I put forward this opinion, which years later he would put forward in a book. He barely listened to me. Suddenly, he said, 'If you have been me, how do you explain the fact that you have forgotten your meeting with an elderly gentleman who in 1918 told you that he, too, was Borges?'

I had not considered this difficulty. 'Maybe the event was so strange I chose to forget it,' I answered without much conviction.

Venturing a question, he said shyly, 'What's your memory like?'

I realized that to a boy not yet twenty a man of over seventy was almost in the grave. 'It often approaches forgetfulness,' I said, 'but it still finds what it's asked to find. I study Old English, and I am not at the bottom of the class.'

Our conversation had already lasted too long to be that of a dream. A sudden idea came to me. 'I can prove at once that you are not dreaming me,' I said. 'Listen carefully to this line, which, as far as I know, you've never read.'

Slowly I entoned the famous verse, '*L'hydre-univers tordant son corps écaillé d'astres.*' I felt his almost fearful awe. He repeated the line, low-voiced, savouring each resplendent word.

'It's true,' he faltered. 'I'll never be able to write a line like that.'

Victor Hugo had brought us together.

Before this, I now recall, he had fervently recited that

8

short piece of Whitman's in which the poet remembers a night shared beside the sea when he was really happy.

'If Whitman celebrated that night,' I remarked, 'it's because he desired it and it did not happen. The poem gains if we look on it as the expression of a longing, not the account of an actual happening.'

He stared at me open-mouthed. 'You don't know him!' he exclaimed. 'Whitman is incapable of telling a lie.'

Half a century does not pass in vain. Beneath our conversation about people and random reading and our different tastes, I realized that we were unable to understand each other. We were too similar and too unalike. We were unable to take each other in, which makes conversation difficult. Each of us was a caricature copy of the other. The situation was too abnormal to last much longer. Either to offer advice or to argue was pointless, since, unavoidably, it was his fate to become the person I am.

All at once, I remembered one of Coleridge's fantasies. Somebody dreams that on a journey through paradise he is given a flower. On awaking, he finds the flower. A similar trick occurred to me. 'Listen,' I said. 'Have you any money?'

'Yes,' he replied. 'I have about twenty francs. I've invited Simon Jichlinski to dinner at the Crocodile tonight.'

'Tell Simon that he will practise medicine in Carouge and that he will do much good. Now, give me one of your coins.'

He drew out three large silver pieces and some small change. Without understanding, he offered me a five-franc coin. I handed him one of those not very sensible American bills that, regardless of their value, are all the same size. He examined it avidly.

'It can't be,' he said, his voice raised. 'It bears the date 1964. All this is a miracle, and the miraculous is terrifying.

9

Witnesses to the resurrection of Lazarus must have been horrified.'

We have not changed in the least, I thought to myself. Ever the bookish reference. He tore up the bill and put his coins away. I decided to throw mine into the river. The arc of the big silver disk losing itself in the silver river would have conferred on my story a vivid image, but luck would not have it so. I told him that the supernatural, if it occurs twice, ceases to be terrifying. I suggested that we plan to see each other the next day, on this same bench, which existed in two times and in two places. He agreed at once and, without looking at his watch, said that he was late. Both of us were lying and we each knew it of the other. I told him that someone was coming for me.

'Coming for you?' he said.

'Yes. When you get to my age, you will have lost your eyesight almost completely. You'll still make out the colour yellow and lights and shadows. Don't worry. Gradual blindness is not a tragedy. It's like a slow summer dusk.'

We said goodbye without having once touched each other. The next day, I did not show up. Neither would he.

I have brooded a great deal over that meeting, which until now I have related to no one. I believe I have discovered the key. The meeting was real, but the other man was dreaming when he conversed with me, and this explains how he was able to forget me; I conversed with him while awake, and the memory of it still disturbs me.

The other man dreamed me, but he did not dream me exactly. He dreamed, I now realize, the date on the dollar bill.

Ulrike

He took the sword Gram and laid it naked between them.

The Saga of the Volsungs, 29

My story will be true to reality or, in any case, to my personal memory of reality, which amounts to the same thing. The events took place only a short time ago, but I know that literary habit is also the habit of adding circumstantial details and of underlining high points. I want to give an account of my meeting with Ulrike (I never knew her surname and perhaps never shall) in the city of York. The narrative will encompass one night and a morning.

It would be easy to say that I saw her for the first time by the Five Sisters of York Minster, those stained-glass windows which, pure of any image, Cromwell's iconoclasts respected, but the fact is that we met in the small lounge of The Northern Inn, which lies outside the city walls. We were a handful, and Ulrike stood with her back to us. Someone offered her a drink and she refused it.

'I am a feminist,' she said. 'I am not out to ape men. I dislike their tobacco and their alcohol.'

The remark was meant to be witty, and I guessed that this was not the first time she had delivered it. I later found out that it was not typical of her, but what we say is not always like us. She mentioned that she had arrived at the museum too late, but that they let her in when they learned she was a Norwegian.

One of those present remarked, 'It's not the first time the Norwegians have entered York.'

'That's right,' she said. 'England was once ours and we lost it – if one can have anything or if anything can be lost.'

It was at this point that I looked at her. A line in Blake speaks of girls of mild silver or of furious gold, but in Ulrike were both gold and mildness. She was tall and slender, with sharp features and grey eyes. Less than by her face, I was impressed by her air of calm mystery. She smiled easily, and the smile seemed to withdraw her from the company. She was dressed in black, which is strange for northern lands, which try to liven the drab surroundings with vivid colours. She spoke a crisp, precise English, rolling her r's slightly. I am not much of an observer; these things I discovered bit by bit.

We were introduced. I told her that I was a professor at the University of the Andes, in Bogotá. I explained that I was a Colombian.

She asked me in a thoughtful way, 'What does it mean to be a Colombian?'

'I don't know,' I replied. 'It's an act of faith.'

'Like being Norwegian,' she affirmed.

I can remember no more of what was said that night. The next day, I came down to the dining room early. Through the windows I saw that it had snowed; in the early morning light the moors faded away. We were the only ones there. Ulrike invited me to her table. She told me that she liked going out for solitary walks.

Recalling a joke of Schopenhauer's, I said, 'So do I. The two of us could go out together.'

We walked away from the inn on the new-fallen snow. There was not a soul about. I suggested that we go on to Thorgate, a few miles down the river. I know that I was already in love with Ulrike; I could never have wanted any other person by my side.

All at once, I heard the distant howling of a wolf. I had never before heard a wolf howl, but I knew it was a wolf. Ulrike was impassive.

A while later she said, as if thinking aloud, 'The few poor swords I saw yesterday in York Minster moved me more than the great ships in the Oslo museum.'

Our paths had crossed. That evening Ulrike would continue her journey on to London; I to Edinburgh.

'In Oxford Street,' she told me, 'I shall follow De Quincey's footsteps in search of his Ann, lost amid the crowds of London.'

'De Quincey stopped looking for her,' I replied. 'All my life, I never have.'

'Maybe you've found her,' Ulrike said, her voice low.

I realized that an unexpected thing was not forbidden me, and I kissed her on the mouth and eyes. She drew away firmly but gently and then declared, 'I'll be yours in the inn at Thorgate. Until then, I ask you not to touch me. It is better that way.'

To a bachelor well along in years, the offer of love is a gift no longer expected. The miracle has a right to impose conditions. I thought back on my youth in Popayán and on a girl in Texas, as fair and slender as Ulrike, who once denied me her love.

I did not make the mistake of asking Ulrike whether she loved me. I realized that this was not her first time nor would it be her last. The adventure, perhaps my last, would be one of many for that splendid, determined follower of Ibsen. Hand in hand, we walked on.

'All this is like a dream, and I never dream,' I said.

'Like that king who never dreamed until a wizard made him sleep in a pigsty,' Ulrike replied. Then she added, 'Listen. A bird is about to sing.'

A moment or two later we heard the song.

'In these lands,' I said, 'it's thought that a person about to die sees into the future.'

'And I am about to die,' she said.

I looked at her in astonishment. 'Let's cut through the woods,' I urged. 'We'll reach Thorgate sooner.'

'The woods are dangerous,' she said.

We continued along the moors.

'I should like this moment to last forever,' I murmured.

'"Forever" is a word forbidden to men,' Ulrike said and, to soften the force of this, she asked me to repeat my name, which she had not caught.

'Javier Otálora,' I said.

She tried to pronounce it and couldn't. I failed, equally, with the name Ulrike.

'I shall call you Sigurd,' she said with a smile.

'If I am Sigurd,' I replied, 'you will be Brynhild.'

She had slowed her step.

'Do you know the saga?' I asked.

'Of course,' she said. 'The tragic story spoiled by the Germans with their late Nibelungs.'

Not wishing to argue the point, I answered, 'Brynhild, you're walking as if you wished a sword lay between us in bed.'

Suddenly we stood before the inn. It did not surprise me that, like the other one, it was called The Northern Inn.

From the top of the stairs, Ulrike called down to me, 'Did you hear the wolf? There are no longer any wolves in England. Hurry.'

Climbing to the upper floor, I noticed that the walls were papered in the style of William Morris, in a deep red, with a design of fruit and birds intertwined. Ulrike went on ahead. The dark room was low, with a slanted ceiling. The awaited bed was duplicated in a dim mirror, and the polished mahogany reminded me of the looking glass of Scriptures. Ulrike had already undressed. She called me by my real name – Javier. I felt that the snow was falling faster. Now there were no longer any mirrors or furniture. There was no sword between us. Time passed like the sands. In the darkness, centuries old, love flowed, and for the first and last time I possessed Ulrike's image.

The Congress

> ... ils s'acheminèrent vers un château immense, au frontispice duquel on lisait: 'Je n'appartiens à personne et j'appartiens à tout le monde. Vous y étiez avant que d'y entrer, et vous y serez encore quand vous en sortirez.'
>
> – Diderot, *Jacques le Fataliste et son Maître*

Buenos Aires, 1955

Alejandro Ferri is my name. Martial echoes may be heard in it, but neither the metals of glory nor the great shadow of the Macedonian – the words belong to the poet of *The Marble Pillars*, who honoured me with his friendship – has any kinship with the nearly anonymous man who strings together these lines on the upper floor of a hotel on Santiago del Estero Street, on the south side of town, which is no longer the old Southside. Any day now, I'll turn seventy-one or seventy-two; I am still teaching English to a handful of students. Out of indecision or carelessness, or for some other reason, I never married, and now I live alone. Loneliness does not worry me; life is difficult enough, putting up with yourself and with your own habits. I realize I am getting on in years. An unmistakable symptom of this is the fact that novelties – maybe because I feel they hold nothing essentially new and are really no more than timid variations – neither interest nor distract me. When I was a young man, I was fond of sunsets, the city's sprawling slums, and of unhappiness; now I prefer mornings and downtown and peace. I no longer play at being Hamlet. I have become a member of the Conservative Party and of a chess club, which I usually attend as an onlooker – sometimes an absentminded onlooker. Anyone who is curious may dig up from some out-of-the-way nook of the National Library, on Mexico Street, a copy of my *Short Study of John Wilkins' Analytical Language*, a work that sadly stands in need of a new edition, if only to correct or to lessen its many mistakes. The library's new director, I am told, is a literary man who dedicates himself to the study of ancient languages (as if modern ones were not sufficiently rudimentary) and to the demagogic exaltation of an imaginary Buenos Aires of knife fighters. I have never cared to meet him. I came to this city in 1899, and only once did chance bring me face to face with a knife fighter or with an individual who had a reputation as such. Further on, should the occasion present itself, I shall relate the episode.

I have already said that I live alone. Several days ago, a fellow-roomer, who had heard me speak of Fermín Eguren, told me that he had died in Punta del Este.

The death of this man, who was certainly never a friend of mine, has unaccountably saddened me. I know that I am alone; I know that in the whole world I am the only keeper of that secret event – the Congress – whose memory I can no longer share. I am now the last member of that Congress. It is undeniable that all men are members of that Congress – that there is not a single being on earth who is not – but I know I am a member in a very different way. I *know* that I am, and that's what sets me apart from my numberless colleagues, present and future. It is undeniable that on the seventh of February, 1904, we swore by what is most holy (is there anything holy on earth, or anything that is not?) never to reveal the history of the Congress, but it is no less undeniable that my now committing perjury is also part of the Congress. This last statement is sufficiently dim, but it may whet the curiosity of my eventual readers.

At any rate, the task I have taken upon myself is not an easy one. I have never before attempted the art of narration – not even in its epistolary form – and, what is doubtless even more important, the story itself is unbelievable. The pen of José Fernández Irala, the undeservedly forgotten author of *The Marble Pillars*, was the one destined for this work, but now it is too late. I shall not deliberately falsify the real facts, although I foresee that laziness and incompetence will more than once lead me into error.

Exact dates are of no account. Let it be recalled that I came from Santa Fe, my native province, in 1899. I have never gone back. I have grown accustomed to Buenos Aires, a city I am not fond of, in the same way that a man grows accustomed to his own body or to an old ailment. Without much caring, I am aware that I am going to die soon; I must, consequently, control my digressive tendencies and get on with my story.

The years do not change our essential selves – if one has an essential self. The impulse that would one night lead me to the Congress of the World was the same that first brought me to the staff of *Última Hora*. To a poor boy from the provinces, becoming a newspaperman was a romantic fate, just as to a poor city boy the life of a gaucho or a farmhand is romantic. I feel no shame at having once wanted to be a journalist, an occupation that now seems trivial to me. I remember having heard my colleague Fernández Irala say that newspapermen wrote for oblivion but that his ambition was to write for time and for memory. He had already chiselled (the verb was then in common use) some of those perfect sonnets that were later to reappear, with one or two minor touches, in the pages of *The Marble Pillars*.

I cannot quite recall the first time I heard the Congress spoken of. Maybe it was on that same evening the cashier paid me my first month's salary and, to celebrate this proof that Buenos Aires had taken me to its bosom, I suggested to Irala that we dine together. He excused himself, saying he could not miss the Congress. I understood at once that he was not referring to the rather pompous, domed building at the foot of an avenue peopled by Spaniards but to something more secret and far more important. People spoke of the Congress, some with open scorn, others with lowered voices, still others with alarm or curiosity – all, I believe, without knowing anything about it. A few Saturdays later, Irala invited me to go along with him.

It must have been nine or ten o'clock at night. On our way, in a streetcar, he told me these preliminary meetings took place every Saturday and that don Alejandro Glencoe, the president of the Congress, perhaps struck by my name, had already signed his approval of my attendance. We went to the Gas-Lamp Coffee House. Some fifteen or twenty members of the Congress sat around a long table; I don't know if there was a dais or if memory adds it. I immediately recognized the president, whom I had never seen before. Don Alejandro was a gentleman, already well along in years, with a high forehead and thinning hair, grey eyes, and a greying reddish beard. I always saw him dressed in a dark frock coat, and he usually held his hands locked together over the head of his cane. He was portly and tall. To his left sat a much younger man, also with red hair. Its violent colour suggested fire, while the colour of Mr Glencoe's beard suggested autumn leaves. To his right was a long-faced young man with an unusually low forehead and dressed like a dandy. Everyone had ordered coffee, and several absinthe. What first caught my attention was the presence of a woman – the only woman among so many men. At the other end of the table sat a boy of about ten, dressed in a sailor suit, who was not long in falling asleep.

There were also a Protestant minister, two unmistakable Jews, and a Negro, who, with a white silk handkerchief around his neck and very tight-fitting clothes, was dressed like a street-corner hoodlum. In front of the Negro and the boy were cups of chocolate. I do not remember any of the other people except for a Mr Marcelo del Mazo, a man of great politeness and fine conversation, whom I never saw again. (I still have a faded, poorly done photograph of one of the gatherings, but I shall not publish it, since the dress, the long hair, and the moustaches of that period would make the whole thing look burlesque and even shabby.)

All groups tend to create their own dialects and rites; the Congress, which always had something dreamlike about it, seemed to want its members to discover – at leisure and for themselves – its real aim and even the names and surnames of its members. I was not long in realizing that I was duty-bound not to ask questions, and I refrained even from asking any of Fernández Irala, who never told me a thing. I did not miss a single Saturday, but a good month or two went by before I reached this understanding. From the second meeting on, my neighbour was Donald Wren, an engineer on the Southern Railways, who was to give me English lessons.

Don Alejandro spoke very little. The rest did not address themselves directly to him, but I felt that their words were meant for him and that everyone was after his approval. One gesture of his slow hand was enough to change the topic of discussion. I came to find out, little by little, that the red-haired man to his left bore the strange name of Twirl. I remember that fragile look of his, which, as though their stature made them dizzy and forced them to hunch forward, is characteristic of some very tall people. His hand, I recall, often played with a copper compass case, which from time to time he set on the table. At the end of 1914, he was killed as an infantryman in an Irish regiment. The person who always sat to the right, the young man with the low forehead, was Fermín Eguren, the president's nephew.

Putting no faith in the methods of realism (a most artificial school if there ever was one), I shall declare right off what I learned only little by little. Beforehand, I want to remind the reader of my situation at the time. I was a poor boy from Casilda, a farmer's son, who had come to the capital and suddenly found himself – this was the way I felt – in the intimate heart of Buenos Aires and perhaps (who knows?) of the whole world. After half a century, I still feel those first dazzling moments, which certainly were not to be the last.

Here are the facts. I shall tell them as briefly as I can. Don Alejandro Glencoe, the president, was an Uruguayan rancher and owner of a large spread of land bordering on Brazil. His father, a native of Aberdeen, had established himself on this continent around the middle of the last century. He brought with him some hundred books – the only books, I venture to say, that don Alejandro read in the course of his life. (I speak of these assorted books, which I have had in my hands, because in one of them lies the root of my story.) The elder Mr Glencoe, on dying, left a daughter and a son. The son was later to become our president; the daughter married an Eguren and was Fermín's mother. Don Alejandro at one time aspired to the Uruguayan National Congress, but the political bosses barred his way. Rankled, he decided to found another Congress and on a vaster scale. He remembered having read in the volcanic pages of Carlyle the fate of Anacharsis Clootz, that worshipper of the goddess Reason who, at the head of thirty-six foreigners, addressed a Paris assembly as 'mankind's spokesman'. Moved by this example, don Alejandro conceived the idea of calling together a Congress of the World that would represent all men of all nations. The centre for the preliminary meetings was the Gas-Lamp Coffee House; the formal act of inauguration, which would take place within some four years, would be held at don Alejandro's ranch. Like so many Uruguayans, don Alejandro – who was no lover of Uruguay's now national hero, Artigas – was fond of Buenos Aires, but he nonetheless decided that the Congress must eventually meet in his own country. Oddly enough, the four-year planning period was carried out with a precision that was almost magical.

In the beginning, we were paid a considerable sum as a per diem, but the zeal that enflamed us prompted Fernández Irala – who was as poor as I was – to renounce his, and all the rest of us followed suit. This measure was healthy, since it served to separate the wheat from the chaff; the number of members was reduced, and only the faithful remained. The one paid position was that of the secretary, Nora Erfjord, who lacked other means of support and whose work at the same time was staggering. To set up a worldwide organization is no trifling enterprise. Letters came and went, and so did cables and telegrams. Potential delegates wrote from Peru, Denmark, and India. A Bolivian wrote that his country's lack of access to the sea should be a matter of prime consideration in our first meetings. Twirl, who had a farseeing mind, remarked that the Congress involved a problem of a philosophical nature. Planning an assembly to represent all men was like fixing the exact number of platonic types – a puzzle that had taxed the imagination of thinkers for centuries. Twirl suggested that, without going farther afield, don Alejandro Glencoe might represent not only cattlemen but also Uruguayans, and also humanity's great forerunners, and also men with red beards, and also those who are seated in armchairs. Nora Erfjord was Norwegian. Would she represent secretaries, Norwegian womanhood, or – more obviously – all beautiful women?

Would a single engineer be enough to represent all engineers – including those of New Zealand?

It was then, I believe, that Fermín broke in. 'Ferri represents the gringos,' he said in a flood of laughter.

Don Alejandro looked at him severely and, in an even voice, said, 'Mr Ferri is representative of the immigrants whose labour is building up this country.'

Fermín Eguren never could bear the sight of me. He took pride in an assortment of things: in being Uruguayan; in coming from old stock; in attracting women; in having chosen an expensive tailor; and, God knows why, in his Basque origin – a people who throughout history have done little else than milk cows.

An incident of the most trivial sort sealed our enmity. After one of the meetings, Eguren suggested that we pay a visit to one of the Junín Street brothels. The plan did not attract me, but, in order not to make myself the butt of his jokes, I accepted. We went with Fernández Irala. On leaving the establishment, we ran into a huge specimen of a man. Eguren, who may have been a bit drunk, gave him a shove. The stranger quickly barred our way and told us, 'Whoever wants to leave is going to have to pass by this knife.'

I remember the glint of the blade in the darkness of the long entranceway. Eguren drew back, visibly afraid. I wasn't too sure of myself, but my hatred got the best of my fright. I reached into my armpit, as if to draw out a weapon, and said in a firm voice, 'We'll settle this out on the street.'

The stranger answered – with another voice now, 'That's the kind of man I like. I wanted to test you, friend.' Then he began to laugh in a cordial way.

'As to "friend",' I answered him, 'that's what you think.' The three of us made our way past him.

The man with the knife entered the brothel. I heard later that his name was Tapia, or Paredes, or something of the kind, and that he had a reputation for brawling. Out on the sidewalk, Irala, who had kept cool, slapped me on the back and said, impressively, 'Among us three, we had a musketeer. Hail, d'Artagnan!'

Fermín Eguren never forgave me for having witnessed his backing down.

I feel that now, and only now, my story begins. The preceding pages have set down no more than the conditions that chance or fate required so that the unbelievable event – perhaps the single event of my whole life – might take place. Don Alejandro Glencoe was always at the centre of the Congress, but over a period of time we felt, not without misgiving, that the real president was Twirl. This singular character, with the flaming moustache, fawned on Glencoe and even on Fermín Eguren – but in such an exaggerated way that those present would think he was actually mocking the two. By so doing, he never once compromised his integrity. Glencoe laboured under the pride of his vast fortune; Twirl discovered that in order to get anything done it was enough to suggest that its cost might prove beyond the president's means. It is my suspicion that at the outset the Congress had been nothing more than a haphazard sort of name. Twirl was continually proposing new areas of expansion, and don Alejandro always accepted. It was like being at the middle of a spreading circle, which grows ever larger and always farther away. Twirl said, for example, that the Congress could not get along without a reference library, and Nierenstein, who worked in a bookshop, went about ordering us the atlases of Justus Perthes and several extensive encyclopedias – all the way from Pliny's *Natural History* and Beauvais' *Speculum* down to the pleasant mazes (I reread these words with Fernández Irala's voice) of the illustrious French Encyclopedists, of the Britannica, of Pierre Larousse, of Brockhaus, of Larsen, and of

Montaner y Simón. I recall how I reverently fondled the silky volumes of a certain Chinese encyclopedia whose finely brushed characters seemed to me more mysterious than the spots on a leopard's skin. As yet, I will say nothing of what lay in store for them and which certainly I do not regret.

Don Alejandro, maybe because we were the only ones who did not try to flatter him, had grown quite fond of Fernández Irala and me. He invited us to spend a few days at his ranch, La Caledonia, where he had a crew of stonemasons already at work.

At the end of a long trip upriver by steamer and a ferry crossing on a raft, we set foot one morning on the Uruguay shore. We then had to spend successive nights in run-down country saloons, while opening and shutting dozens of gateways all day along back roads in the Cuchilla Negra. We made our way in a light carriage; the countryside seemed wider and lonelier to me than the small farm where I was born.

I still hold my two images of the ranch – the one I brought with me and the one my eyes finally saw. Absurdly, I had imagined, as in a dream, an impossible combination of the flat plains of Santa Fe and of the rather gaudy Victorian Buenos Aires Waterworks. La Caledonia was a long adobe building with a thatched saddle roof and a brick-paved gallery. It appeared to be built for hardship and endurance. The rough walls were nearly a yard thick and the doors were narrow. Nobody had ever thought of planting a tree. The sun's first and last rays beat down on the place. The corrals were of stone; the cattle were many, scrawny and long-horned; the horses' switching tails reached the ground. For the first time in my life, I knew the taste of freshly slaughtered meat. Some sacks of sea biscuit were brought out; a few days later, the foreman told me he had never eaten bread in his life. Irala asked where the bathroom was, and, with a sweeping gesture, don Alejandro indicated the entire continent. It was a moonlit night; I went out to stretch my legs, and I surprised Irala being watched by an ostrich.

The heat, which the night had not dispelled, was unbearable, and everyone praised the coolness. The rooms were low-ceilinged and many, and seemed to me barely furnished; we were given one, facing south, in which there were two cots and a dresser with a silver washbasin and pitcher. The floor was dirt.

The second day, I came across the library and the volumes of Carlyle, and I found the pages dedicated to mankind's spokesman, Anacharsis Clootz, who had led me to that morning and to that loneliness. After breakfast, which was identical with dinner, don Ajelandro showed us the building under construction. We rode three or four miles on horseback out in the wide open. Irala, whose horsemanship was shaky, had an accident; unsmiling, the foreman remarked, 'You Argentines really know how to dismount.'

From way off, we could see the construction site. Some twenty men were at work building a kind of tumbledown amphitheatre. I recall a series of stages and ladders and stone tiers with stretches of sky showing between.

More than once, I tried to speak with the gauchos, but my efforts failed. In some way, they knew they were different. Among themselves, they used a spare, guttural Brazilianized Spanish. It was obvious that both Indian and Negro blood ran in their veins. They were short and strong; at La Caledonia, I became a tall man – something that had never happened to me until then.

Almost all of them dressed with their legs wrapped in the *chiripá*, and a few wore the wide, baggy *bombachas*. They had little or nothing in common with the complaining heroes found in the books of Hernández or of Rafael Obligado. Under the stimulus of Saturday-night alcohol, they were easily moved to violence. There wasn't a single woman around, and I never once heard a guitar.

I was more interested in the change that had come over don Alejandro than I was in these border-country men. In Buenos Aires, he was a pleasant, reserved gentleman; at La Caledonia, like his fathers before him, he became the stern chief of a clan. Sunday mornings, he read Holy Scripture to the hands, who did not understand a single word. One night, the foreman, a youngish man who had inherited the job from his father, reported to us that one of the day labourers and one of the regular help were having it out with knives. Don Alejandro got up, unruffled. When he came to the circle of onlookers, he drew out the weapon he always carried, handed it to the foreman (who appeared to me to cringe), and stepped between the knives. At once, I heard the order, 'Drop those knives, boys.' With the same calm voice, he added, 'Now shake hands and behave yourselves. I don't want any brawling around here.'

The two men obeyed. The next day, I learned that don Alejandro had fired the foreman.

I felt the loneliness ringing me in, and I began fearing I'd never get back to Buenos Aires. I wonder whether Fernández Irala shared that fear. We talked a lot about Argentina and what we'd do when we returned. I missed the stone lions of a certain gateway on Jujuy Street, near the Plaza del Once, and the light of a particular old bar in some dim part of town, but not my familiar haunts. Always a good rider, I fell into the habit of going out on horseback and riding long distances. I still remember the particular piebald I used to saddle up myself. On some afternoon or on some night or other, I probably was in Brazil, since the border was nothing but a line traced out by widely spaced markers. Then, at the close of a day exactly like all the rest, don Alejandro told us, 'We'll turn in early. Tomorrow we'll be off while it's still cool.'

Once down the river, I felt so happy that I was even able to think back to La Caledonia with affection.

We took up our Saturday meetings again. At the first one, Twirl asked for the floor. He said, with his usual flowers of rhetoric, that the library of the Congress of the World could not be limited to reference books alone, and that the classical works of all nations and all languages were a veritable storehouse that we could not safely afford to ignore. The suggestion was approved on the spot; Fernández Irala and Dr Ignacio Cruz, who was a teacher of Latin, accepted the job of selecting the appropriate texts. Twirl had already talked things over with Nierenstein.

In those days, there wasn't a single Argentine whose utopia was not Paris. Perhaps the most enthusiastic of us was Fermín Eguren; next, for quite different reasons, came Fernández Irala. To the poet of *The Marble Pillars*, Paris was Verlaine and Leconte de Lisle, while to Eguren it was an improved version of Junín Street. I suspect that he had come to some understanding with Twirl. At a subsequent meeting, Twirl brought up the question of what language the members of the Congress would use, arguing the feasibility of sending delegates to London and Paris to gather information. Feigning impartiality, he first put up my name, and then, as an apparent afterthought, that of his friend Eguren. As always, don Alejandro agreed.

I think I have written that, in exchange for some lessons in Italian, Wren had initiated me into the study of the inexhaustible English language. As far as possible, we did away with grammar and with those exercises concocted for the beginner, and we found our way directly into poetry, whose forms demand brevity. My first contact with the language that was to fill out my life was Stevenson's brave 'Requiem'. Then came the ballads that Percy revealed to the dignified eighteenth century. A short while before leaving for London, I was dazzled by Swinburne – an experience that made me begin to doubt (and to feel guilty about it) the eminence of Irala's alexandrines.

I reached London early in January, 1902; I remember the soft touch of falling snow, which I had never before seen and for which I was grateful. Luckily, Eguren and I had travelled separately. I roomed at a modest boarding house behind the British Museum, where mornings and afternoons I studied in the library in search of a language worthy of the Congress of the World. I did not overlook universal languages, investigating both Esperanto – which Lugones qualifies as 'impartial, simple, and economical' – and Volapük, which, declining verbs and conjugating nouns, attempts to work out all linguistic possibilities. I also weighed the arguments in favour of and against the revival of Latin, a nostalgia for which has endured down through the centuries. I even dwelled on an examination of John Wilkins' analytical language, in which the definition of each word is to be found in the letters that spell it out. It was beneath the high dome of the reading room that I first met Beatrice.

This is meant to be a general history of the Congress of the World, not of Alejandro Ferri, but the former takes in the latter, just as it takes in all other histories. Beatrice was tall, trim, with fine features and a head of red hair that might have reminded me – but never did – of the shady Twirl. She was not yet twenty. She had come down from one of the northern counties to study literature at the university. Her background, like mine, was humble. At that time, to be of Italian stock in Buenos Aires was still to be looked down on, but in London I found out that being Italian was to many people a romantic attribute. Within a few evenings, we were lovers; I asked her to marry me, but Beatrice Frost, like Nora Erfjord, was a follower of the faith preached by Ibsen, and she did not

28

want to tie herself down to anyone. From her lips came the word I never dared speak. O nights, O darkness warm and shared, O love that flows in shadows like some secret river, O that instant of ecstasy when each is both, O that ecstasy's purity and innocence, O the coupling in which we became lost so as then to lose ourselves in sleep, O the first light of dawn, and I watching her.

On the rough Brazil border, I had been plagued by homesickness; not so in London's red labyrinth, which gave me so many things. Despite the pretexts I dreamed up to delay my departure, I had to return home at the end of the year. Beatrice and I celebrated Christmas together. I assured her that don Alejandro would invite her to join the Congress; she answered, in an offhand way, that she had always wanted to visit the Southern Hemisphere, and that a cousin of hers, a dentist, had settled in Tasmania.

Beatrice did not want to come to the boat. Goodbyes, to her way of thinking, were too dramatic, were a senseless feast of unhappiness, and she detested dramatics. We parted in the library, where we had met the winter before. As a man, I'm a coward; to avoid the anguish of waiting for letters, I did not leave her my address.

Return trips are shorter, I have always noticed, but that crossing of the Atlantic, heavy with memories and anxieties, seemed unusually long. Nothing hurt me as much as thinking that, in a parallel with my life, Beatrice would go on living hers, minute by minute and night by night. I wrote a lengthy letter, destroying it as we left Montevideo. When I reached Argentina – it was on a Thursday – Irala was waiting for me at the dock. I went back to my old place on Chile Street; that day and the next he and I spent together talking and taking long walks. I wanted to recover Buenos Aires again. It was a relief to find out that Fermín Eguren was staying on in Paris; I knew the fact of my having come back before him would in some way make up for my long absence.

Irala was downcast. Fermín was squandering huge sums in Europe and had more than once disobeyed the order to return home. This was to have been foreseen. I was more disturbed by other news. Twirl, in spite of the opposition of Irala and Cruz, had invoked the Younger Pliny, according to whom there is no book so bad it does not contain some good, and had proposed the indiscriminate purchase of bound volumes of the daily press, of thirty-four hundred copies of *Don Quixote* in various edtions, of the complete works of General Mitre, of Ph.D. theses, of old account books, of bulletins, and of theatre programmes. Everything gives witness, he had said. Nierenstein backed him; don Alejandro, 'after three resounding Saturdays' (as Irala put it), approved the motion. Nora Erfjord had resigned her position as secretary; it was taken over by a new member, Karlinski, who was a tool of Twirl's. The bulky packages began piling up now, without files or catalogues, in the back rooms and in the wine cellar of don Alejandro's rambling old town house. Early in July, Irala spent a week back at La Caledonia, where the masons had broken off their work. The foreman, upon questioning, explained that that was what the boss had ordered, and that there would always be time enough tomorrow.

In London, I had drafted a report that there is now no point in going into. That Friday, I went to pay a visit to don Alejandro and to deliver a copy of what I had written. Fernández Irala came with me. It was early evening, and the cold south wind blew into the house. At the front gate, on Alsina Street, a delivery wagon, pulled by three horses, stood waiting. I remember that the deliverymen were weighed down under the loads they went about piling up in the last patio. Twirl was imperious, giving them orders. Also present, indoors, as if they had

had an inkling of something, were Nora Erfjord and Nierenstein and Cruz and Donald Wren and a few other members of the Congress. Nora threw her arms around me and kissed me, and that embrace and that kiss made me remember others. The Negro, brimming over with good nature and happiness, kissed my hand.

In one of the rooms, the square trapdoor to the cellar was wide open; some masonry steps plunged down into darkness. Suddenly we heard footsteps. Before laying eyes on him, I knew it was don Alejandro. He came almost on the run.

His voice was different. It was not the voice of the deliberate gentleman who presided over our Saturdays, nor that of the feudal landowner who had put a stop to a knife duel and who preached the word of God to his gauchos – but it seemed more like this latter.

Without looking at anyone, he ordered, 'Get everything out that's packed away down there. I don't want a single book left in that cellar.'

The work went on for nearly an hour. Outside, on the earth floor of the last patio, we made a pile that was taller than the tallest head. All of us marched back and forth; the only person who failed to move was don Alejandro.

Then came the order, 'Now set fire to that heap.'

Twirl went pale. Nierenstein blurted, 'How can the Congress of the World do without this valuable material I've collected with so much love?'

'The Congress of the World?' said don Alejandro. He laughed scornfully. I had never before heard him laugh.

There is a mysterious pleasure in destruction. The flames crackled brightly, and we all had to press back against the walls or move indoors. Darkness, ashes, and an odour of burning were left behind in the patio. I remember some undamaged pages lying white against the ground. Nora Erfjord, who felt for don Alejandro that love which young women often feel for older men, said, without really understanding, 'Don Alejandro knows what he's doing.'

Irala, always true to literature, attempted an epigram. 'Every few centuries,' he said, 'the Library of Alexandria must be burned down.'

Then the revelation was made to us.

'It has taken me four years to understand what I am about to say,' don Alejandro began. 'My friends, the undertaking we have set for ourselves is so vast that it embraces – I now see – the whole world. Our Congress cannot be a group of charlatans deafening each other in the sheds of an out-of-the-way ranch. The Congress of the World began with the first moment of the world and it will go on when we are dust. There's no place on earth where it does not exist. The Congress is the books we've burned. The Congress is Job on the ash heap and Christ on the Cross. The Congress is that worthless boy who squanders my substance on whores.'

I could not hold myself back. 'Don Alejandro,' I broke in, 'I, too, am to blame. I had finished my report, which I now hand you, but I stayed on and on in England, throwing your money away on a woman.'

Don Alejandro went on. 'I had already guessed as much, Ferri. The Congress is my cattle. The Congress is the cattle I have sold and the miles of land that are no longer mine.'

A horror-stricken voice was raised – Twirl's. 'You don't mean to say you've sold La Caledonia?'

'Yes,' don Alejandro said calmly, 'I've sold it. I haven't a square foot of land to my name, but I do not regret it, because now I see things as they are. Perhaps we shall never meet again, for the Congress stands in no need of us. But this last night we will all go out together to see the true Congress.'

Drunk with victory, he overwhelmed us with his resolution and faith. No one – not for a single second – thought he was mad.

In the square, we climbed into an open carriage. I squeezed myself onto the driver's seat beside the coachman, and don Alejandro ordered, 'Maestro, let's have a turn around the city. Take us anywhere you like.'

The Negro, perched on the running board, never stopped smiling. I'll never know whether or not he realized what was going on.

Words are symbols that assume a shared memory. The memory I now want to set down is mine alone; all those who share it have died. The mystics invoke a rose, a kiss, a bird that is all birds, a sun that is all the stars and the sun, a jug of wine, a garden, or the sexual act. Of these metaphors, none will serve me for that long, joyous night, which left us, tired out and happy, at the borders of dawn. We barely spoke while the wheels and the horses' hooves clattered over the cobblestones. Before daybreak, beside a dark, humble body of water that may have been the Maldonado or the Riachuelo, Nora Erfjord's high voice sang the ballad of Sir Patrick Spens, and don Alejandro, in a low voice and out of tune, chimed in with a few verses. The English words did not bring me Beatrice's image. At my back, Twirl muttered, 'I wanted to do evil and I have done good.'

Something of what we glimpsed lives on – the reddish wall of the Recoleta cemetery, the yellow wall of a jail, a couple of men dancing together at a right-angled street corner, a church courtyard with black and white tiles and a grilled iron fence, a railway gate crossing, my house, a marketplace, the damp unfathomable night – but none of these fleeting things, which may have been others, now matter. What really matters is having felt that our plan, which more than once we made a joke of, really and secretly existed and was the world and ourselves. Down through the years, without much hope, I have sought the taste of that night; a few times I thought I had recaptured it in music, in love, in untrustworthy memories, but it has never come back to me except once in a dream. When we swore not to say a word to anyone, it was already Saturday morning.

I never saw any of them again, outside of Irala. He and I never spoke about the Congress; anything we might have said would have been a desecration. In 1914, don Alejandro Glencoe died and was buried in Montevideo. Irala had already passed away the year before.

Once, I ran across Nierenstein on Lima Street, and we pretended not to see each other.

There are more things

To the memory of H. P. Lovecraft

On the point of taking my last examination at the University of Texas, in Austin, I learned that my uncle Edwin Arnett had died of an aneurysm at the far end of the South American continent. I felt what we all feel when someone dies – the remorse, now pointless, for not having been kinder. We forget that we are all dead men conversing with dead men. My course of study was philosophy. I remembered that it was my uncle, at the Casa Colorada, his home near Lomas, on the edge of Buenos Aires, who, without invoking a single proper name, had first revealed to me philosophy's beautiful perplexities. One of the after-dinner oranges was his aid in initiating me into Berkeley's idealism; a chessboard was enough to illustrate the paradoxes of the Eleatics. Years later, he was to lend me Hinton's treatises which attempt to demonstrate the reality of four-dimensional space and which the reader is meant to imagine by means of complicated exercises with multicoloured cubes. I shall never forget the prisms and pyramids that we erected on the floor of his study.

My uncle was an engineer. Before retiring from his job with the railroad, he decided to build himself a house in Turdera, which offered the advantages of almost country-like solitude and of proximity to the city. Nothing was more predictable than that the architect should be his close friend Alexander Muir. This uncompromising man followed the uncompromising teachings of John Knox. My uncle, like almost all the gentlemen of his day, had been a freethinker or, rather, an agnostic, but he was interested in theology, just as he was interested in Hinton's unreal cubes and in the well-constructed nightmares of the young H. G. Wells. He liked dogs, and he had a great sheepdog that he had named Samuel Johnson, in memory of Lichfield, his far-off birthplace.

The Casa Colorada stood on a height of land, bordered on the west by sun-blackened fields. Inside its fence, the araucarias did nothing to soften its air of gloom. Instead of a flat roof, there was a slate-tiled saddle roof and a square tower with a clock. These seemed to oppress the walls and the meagre windows. As a boy, I used to accept all this ugliness, just as one accepts those incompatible things which, only because they coexist, are called the world.

I returned home in 1921. To avoid legal complications, the house had been auctioned off. It was bought by a foreigner, a Max Preetorius, who paid double what was offered by the highest bidder. No sooner was the deed signed than he arrived, late one afternoon, with two helpers and they carted off to a rubbish dump, not far from the old Drover's Road, all the furniture, all the books, and all the utensils of the house. (I sadly recalled the diagrams in the Hinton volumes and the great globe.) The next day, Preetorius went to Muir and proposed certain alterations that the architect indignantly rejected. In the end, a firm from Buenos Aires took charge of the work. The local carpenters refused to furnish the house again. Finally, a certain Mariani, from Glew, accepted the conditions laid down by Preetorius. For an entire fortnight he had to labour by night behind closed doors. It was also by night that the new owner of the Casa Colorada moved in. The windows no longer opened, but chinks of light could be made out in the dark. One morning, the milkman found the sheepdog dead on the walk, headless and mutilated. That winter they felled the araucarias. Nobody saw Preetorius again.

News of these events, as may be imagined, left me uneasy. I know that my most obvious trait is curiosity – that same curiosity that brought me together with a woman completely different from me only in order to find out who she was and what she was like, to take up (without appreciable results) the use of laudanum, to explore transfinite numbers, and to undertake the hideous adventure that I am about to tell. Ominously, I decided to look into the matter.

My first step was to see Alexander Muir. I remembered him as tall-standing and dark, with a wiry build that suggested strength. Now the years had stooped him and his black beard had gone grey. He received me at his Temperley house, which, foreseeably, was like my uncle's, since both houses followed the solid standards of the good poet and bad builder William Morris.

Conversation was spare – Scotland's symbol, after all, is the thistle. I had the feeling, nonetheless, that the strong Ceylon tea and the equally generous plate of scones (which my host broke in two and buttered for me as if I were still a boy) were, in fact, a frugal Calvinistic feast offered to the nephew of his friend. His theological differences with my uncle had been a long game of chess, demanding of each player the collaboration of his opponent.

Time passed and I was no nearer my business. There was an uncomfortable silence and Muir spoke. 'Young man,' he said, 'you have not come all this way to talk about Edwin or the United States, a country that I have little interest in. What's troubling you is the sale of the Casa Colorada and its odd buyer. They do me, too. Frankly, the story displeases me, but I'll tell you what I can. It will not be much.'

After a while he went on, unhurriedly. 'Before Edwin died, the mayor called me into his office. He was with the parish priest. They asked me to draw the plans for a Catholic chapel. My work would be well paid. On the spot, I answered no. I am a servant of God and I cannot commit the abomination of erecting altars to idols.' Here he stopped.

'Is that all?' I finally dared ask.

'No. This whelp of a Jew Preetorius wanted me to destroy my work and in its place get up a monstrous thing. Abomination comes in many shapes.' He pronounced these words gravely and got to his feet.

Outside, on turning the corner, I was approached by Daniel Iberra. We knew one another the way people in small towns do. He suggested that we accompany each other back to Turdera. I have never been keen on hoodlums, and I expected a sordid litany of violent and more or less apocryphal back-room stories, but I gave in and accepted his invitation. It was nearly nightfall. On seeing the Casa Colorada come into view from a few blocks off, Iberra made a detour. I asked him why. His reply was not what I anticipated.

'I am don Felipe's right arm,' he said. 'Nobody has ever called me soft. That young Urgoiti who took the trouble to come looking for me all the way from Merlo – you probably remember what happened to him. Look. A few nights ago, I was returning from a party. A hundred yards or so from that house I saw something. My horse reared up, and if I hadn't had a good grip on him and made him turn down an alley, maybe I wouldn't be telling this story now. What I saw justified the horse's fright.' Angrily, Iberra added a swear word.

That night I did not sleep. Around dawn, I dreamed about an engraving that I had never seen before or that I had seen and forgotten; it was in the style of Piranesi, and it had a labyrinth in it. It was a stone amphitheatre ringed by cypresses, above whose tops it reached. There were neither doors nor windows; rather, it displayed an endless row of narrow vertical slits. With a magnifying glass, I tried to see the Minotaur inside. At last, I made it out. It was a monster of a monster, more bison than bull, and, its human body stretched out on the ground, it seemed to be asleep and dreaming. Dreaming of what or of whom?

That evening, I passed by the Casa Colorada. The iron gate was shut and some of its bars were bent. What once was garden was now overgrown with weeds. To the right, there was a shallow ditch and its outer edges were trampled.

There was only one move left, but for days I kept putting it off – not because I felt it to be altogether a waste, but because it would drag me to the inevitable, to the last.

Without much hope, I went to Glew. Mariani, the carpenter, was a stout, pink-faced Italian, common and cordial and now somewhat advanced in years. A glance at him was enough for me to dismiss the stratagems I had contrived the night before. I handed him my card, which he pompously spelled out aloud with a certain reverential stumbling when he reached the 'Ph.D.' I told him I was interested in the furniture made by him for the house in Turdera that had been my uncle's. The man spoke on and on. I shall not try to transcribe his torrent of words and gestures, but he told me that his motto was to satisfy his customer's every demand, no matter how outlandish it was, and that he had carried out his work to the letter. After rummaging in various drawers he showed me some papers that I could make neither head nor tail of; they were signed by the elusive Preetorius. (Doubtless, Mariani mistook me for a lawyer.) On saying goodbye, he confided to me that even for all the world's gold he would never again set foot in Turdera, let alone that house. He added that the customer is sacred, but that in his humble opinion

39

Mr Preetorius was crazy. Then he grew quiet, obviously repentant. I was unable to worm anything more out of him.

I had allowed for this failure, but it is one thing to allow for something and quite another to see it happen. Time and again, I said to myself that the solution of this enigma did not concern me and that the one true enigma was time, that seamless chain of past, present, and future, of the ever and the never. Such reflections turned out to be useless, however; after whole afternoons devoted to the study of Schopenhauer or Royce, night after night I would walk the dirt roads ringing the Casa Colorada. Sometimes I caught a glimpse upstairs of a very white light; other times, I thought I heard a moaning. It went on this way until the nineteenth of January.

It was one of those Buenos Aires days when a man feels himself not only bullied and insulted by the summer but even debased by it. At around eleven o'clock at night the storm broke. First came the south wind, and then the water in torrents. I wandered about looking for a tree. In the sudden glare of a lightning flash I found myself a few steps from the fence. Whether out of fear or hope I don't know, but I tried the gate. Unexpectedly, it opened. I made my way, pushed along by the storm. Sky and earth threatened me. The door of the house was also open. A squall of rain lashed my face and I went in.

Inside, the floor tiles had been torn up and I stepped on matted grass. A sweet, sickening smell filled the house. Right or left, I'm not sure which, I tripped on a stone ramp. Quickly, I went up. Almost unawares, I turned on the light switch.

The dining room and the library of my memories were now, with the wall between them torn down, a single great bare room containing one or two pieces of furniture. I shall not try to describe them, since I am not altogether sure – in spite of the cruel white light – of having seen them. Let me explain myself. To see a thing one has to comprehend it. An armchair presupposes the human body, its joints and limbs; a pair of scissors, the act of cutting. What can be said of a lamp or a car? The savage cannot comprehend the missionary's Bible; the passenger does not see the same rigging as the sailors. If we really saw the world, maybe we would understand it.

None of the meaningless shapes that that night granted me corresponded to the human figure or, for that matter, to any conceivable use. I felt revulsion and terror. In one of the corners, I found a ladder which led to the upper floor. The spaces between the iron rungs, which were no more than ten, were wide and irregular. That ladder, implying hands and feet, was comprehensible, and in some way this relieved me. I put out the light and waited for some time in the dark. I did not hear the least sound, but the presence there of incomprehensible things disquieted me. In the end, I made up my mind.

Once upstairs, my fearful hand switched on the light a second time. The nightmare that had foreshadowed the lower floor came alive and flowered on the next. Here there were either many objects or a few linked together. I now recall a sort of long operating table, very high and in the shape of a U, with round hollows at each end. I thought that maybe it was the bed of the house's inhabitant, whose monstrous anatomy revealed itself in this way, implicitly, like an animal's or a god's by its shadow. From some page or other of Lucan there came to my lips the word 'amphisbaena', which hinted at, but which certainly did not exhaust, what my eyes were later to see. I also remember a V of mirrors that became lost in the upper darkness.

What would the inhabitant be like? What could it be looking for on this planet, no less hideous to it than it to us? From what secret regions of astronomy or time, from what ancient and now incalculable dusk can it have reached this South American suburb and this particular night?

I felt an intruder in the chaos. Outside, the rain had stopped. I looked at my watch and saw with astonishment that it was almost two o'clock. I left the light on and carefully began climbing down. To get down the way I had come up was not impossible – to get down before the inhabitant returned. I guessed that it had not locked the doors because it did not know how.

My feet were touching the next to last rung of the ladder when I felt that something, slow and oppressive and two-fold, was coming up the ramp. Curiosity overcame my fear, and I did not shut my eyes.

The Sect of the Thirty

The original manuscript may be consulted at the University of Leiden; the text is in Latin, but one or two Hellenisms justify the conjecture that it was translated from the Greek. According to Leisegang, it dates from the fourth century A.D. Gibbon mentions it in passing in one of the footnotes to the fifteenth chapter of his *Decline and Fall*. The anonymous author has recorded:

... The Sect was never large, and now its proselytes number but a scant few. Decimated by sword and fire, they sleep by the wayside or, since it is forbidden them to build any form of dwelling place, among the ruins spared by war. They also journey about quite naked. These facts are common knowledge. My aim here is to leave a written record of what it has been vouchsafed me to discover of the Sect's beliefs and customs. I have argued at length with its masters and have met with little success in converting them to the Faith of Our Lord.

The first thing about the Sect that drew my attention was the variousness of its notions regarding the dead. Among the most ignorant, for example, it is held that the burial of those who have departed this life is entrusted to their spirits; others, the unorthodox, maintain that Jesus' admonition to 'let the dead bury their dead' is meant to condemn the pompous vanity of our funeral rites.

43

The advice to sell what one has and give to the poor is closely followed by every sectarian; those so benefited give to others and these, in turn, to still others. This should suffice to explain their indigence and nakedness, which, in addition, brings them nearer the state of paradise. Fervently they repeat the words, 'Behold the ravens of the air: for they sow not, neither do they reap, nor have they barns or sheds; yet your heavenly Father feedeth them. Are ye not much better than they?' Their teaching forbids all saving: 'Wherefore, if God so clothe the grass of the field, which to day is, and to morrow is cast into the oven, *shall he* not much more *clothe* you, O ye of little faith? Therefore take no thought, saying, What shall we eat? or, What shall we drink?'

The judgement 'whosoever looketh on a woman to lust after her hath committed adultery with her already in his heart' is a piece of straightforward advice about maintaining purity. Yet, many are the members of the Sect who point out that if there is not one man on earth who has not looked upon a woman to lust after her all men have committed adultery. Since the desire is as sinful as the act, the righteous may without risk indulge in the most outrageous lust.

The Sect shuns temples; its elders preach in the open air, from the top of a hill or a wall, or sometimes from a boat on the shore.

The Sect's name has given rise to persistent conjectures. One such suggests that it refers to the number to which the faithful have been reduced, which is ridiculous and yet prophetic, because, due to its perverse set of beliefs, the Sect is destined to die out. Another conjecture is that the name derives from the height of the Ark, which was thirty cubits; another, which distorts the calendar, from the number of nights that make up a lunar month; another, from the Saviour's age at baptism; another, from Adam's years when he rose out of the red dust of the ground. All are equally untrue. No less deceiving is the list of thirty godheads or thrones, of which one is Abraxas, portrayed by a cock's head, the arms and torso of a man, and the tail of an entwined serpent.

The priceless gift of communicating Truth has not been granted me. One knows the Truth but is unable to argue it. May others more gifted than I save the members of the Sect by preaching – by preaching or by fire, for it is better to be put to death than to commit suicide. I shall therefore limit myself to giving an account of the abominable heresy.

The Word was made flesh to become a man among men, who would deliver Him up to the cross and be redeemed by Him. He was born of the womb of a woman of the chosen people not only to preach Love, but to suffer martyrdom.

It was necessary that events be unforgettable. The death of a human being by the sword or by drinking hemlock was not enough to move the imagination of mankind to the end of time. The Lord arranged things in a dramatic way. This accounts for the Last Supper, for Jesus' words that foretold his betrayal, for the repeated warning to one of the disciples, for the blessing of the bread and wine, for Peter's pledges, for the solitary vigil in the garden of Gethsemane, for the sleep of the twelve disciples, for the Son of God's human prayer, for the sweat like blood, for the multitude with swords and staves, for the kiss of betrayal, for Pilate's washing his hands, for the scourging, for the mocking, for the crown of thorns, for the purple robe and reed sceptre, for the vinegar with gall, for the cross on the summit of a hill, for the promise to the repentant thief, for the earth that shook and the darkness over all the land.

Divine Providence, to which I owe so many blessings, has allowed me to discover the real and secret reason for the Sect's name. In Kerioth, where in all likelihood it originated, there survives a conventicle known as the Thirty Coins. This was the earliest name, and it gives us the clue. In the drama of the Cross (I mean this with due reverence) there were intentional and unintentional actors – all of them indispensable, all of them fatal. Unintentional were the priests who handed out the pieces of silver, unintentional was the multitude that asked for Barabbas, unintentional was the Governor of Judea, unintentional were the Roman soldiers who erected the cross of His martyrdom and nailed the nails and cast lots for His garments. The intentional actors were only two – the Redeemer and Judas. The latter cast down the thirty pieces of silver that were the price of Salvation and went and hanged himself. At the time, like the Son of Man, he was thirty-three years old. The Sect worships them equally and absolves all the others. There is no one culprit. Everyone, unwitting or not, is an agent in the scheme laid down by Divine Wisdom. All of them now share the Glory.

My hand trembles to set down yet another abomination. In order to follow the example of their masters, the believers, upon attaining the designated age, have themselves mocked and crucified on the summit of a hill. This criminal violation of the Fifth Commandment must be brought to an end with all the severity that human and divine laws have always demanded. May the curses of the skies, may the hatred of the angels . . .

No more of the manuscript has been unearthed.

The night of the gifts

It was many years ago in the old Confitería del Águila, on Florida Street up around Piedad, that we heard this story. The problem of knowledge was being discussed. Someone invoked the platonic theory that we have already seen everything in a previous world, so that to know is to know again. My father, I believe, said that Bacon had written that if to learn is to remember, not to know is in fact to have forgotten. Another person, a man getting on in years, who was probably a bit lost in metaphysics, decided to enter in. Speaking slowly and deliberately this is what he told us:

Frankly, I don't understand all this talk of platonic archetypes. Nobody remembers the first time he saw the colour yellow or black, or the first time he tasted a certain fruit – maybe because he was small then and had no way of knowing he was initiating a very long series. Of course, there are other first times that no one forgets. I can tell you what a certain night of my life gave me, one I often recall – the night of the thirtieth of April, 1874.

Summer holidays were much longer then, but I don't know why we stayed away from Buenos Aires until that late date. We were at the ranch of some cousins, the Dornas, not far from Lobos. During that time, one of the cowhands, Rufino, initiated me into country things. I was approaching thirteen; he was somewhat older and had a reputation as a daredevil. He was quick, agile. When the younger hands played at knife-fighting with burnt sticks, the one who always got his face marked was Rufino's opponent. One Friday, Rufino suggested we go into town the next night to have a little fun. Of course, I leaped at the chance, but without really knowing what it was all about. I warned him I didn't know how to dance. Dancing was easy to learn, he said.

After dinner on Saturday, at around seven-thirty, we set off. Rufino had rigged himself out like someone going to a party, and he wore a silver knife in his belt. I had a little knife like it, but I didn't bring mine for fear of being laughed at. It was not long before we glimpsed the first houses. I don't suppose any of you has ever been to Lobos. Not that it matters. There's no small town in the Argentine that isn't exactly like all the others – even to the point of thinking itself different. Each has the same unpaved alleys, the same empty lots, the same one-story houses – all of which make a man on horseback seem more important.

We dismounted at a certain street corner in front of a house painted sky-blue or pink, with a sign saying 'La Estrella'. Tied to the hitching post were some horses with good saddles. Through the half-open street door I saw a shaft of light. At the end of the entranceway was a large room with wooden benches on either side and, between the benches, a number of dark doors that opened who knew where. A little mongrel with yellow fur ran up barking to welcome me. Quite a few people were about, and a half dozen or so women in floral dressing gowns came and went. A respectable-looking lady, dressed in black from head to foot, seemed to be the owner of the house. Rufino greeted her, saying, 'I've brought a new friend, but he's not much of a rider.'

'Don't worry,' the woman answered. 'He'll learn soon enough.'

I felt ashamed. To draw their attention away, or to make them see that I was a boy, I began playing with the dog at the end of one of the benches. On a table in the kitchen burned some cheap candles in bottles, and I also remember a small brazier in a corner to the rear. On the whitewashed wall opposite was a picture of Our Lady of Mercy.

Somebody, between one joke and another, was tuning a guitar that gave him a lot of trouble. Out of sheer timidity I did not refuse a gin, which burned my mouth like a red-hot coal. Among the women I noticed one who seemed different from the others. They called her La Cautiva – the Captive. There was something Indian about her, but her features were like a picture and her eyes very sad. Her braided hair reached her waist. Rufino saw that I was looking at her.

'Let's hear about the raid again – to refresh our memories,' he said to her.

The girl spoke as if she were alone, and in some way I felt that she was unable to think of anything else and that the story she told us was the only thing that had happened to her in her life.

'I was very young when they brought me from Catamarca,' she said. 'What did I know about Indian raids? At Santa Irene we didn't even mention such things, we were so scared. As if unravelling a secret, I gradually found out that Indians could descend like a cloud and kill people and steal their stock. Women they carried off into the pampa, and they did everything to them. I tried as hard as I could not to believe any of this. My brother Lucas – the Indians later put a spear through him – swore it was all lies, but when a thing is true it has to be said only once for you to know it's so. The government hands out strong drink and yerba to keep the Indians happy, but they have very clever wizards telling them what to do. At the word of one of their chiefs, it's nothing for them to attack a ranch somewhere out between the forts, which are far apart. Just from thinking about it so much, I almost wished they would come, and I knew how to look for them out towards the setting sun. I don't know how much time went by, but there were frosts and summers and roundups and the death of the foreman's son before the raid.'

She paused for a moment or two, lost in thought, then went on. 'It was as if the south wind brought them. I saw a thistle in a ditch, and that night I dreamed of Indians. It happened at daybreak. The animals knew it before we did – the same as when there's an earthquake. The cattle were restless and birds wheeled in the sky. We ran to look in the direction I always looked.'

'Who warned you?' someone asked.

Distant as ever, the girl repeated her last sentence. 'We ran to look in the direction I always looked. It was as if the whole desert had begun to move. Through the bars of the window grille we saw the cloud of dust before we saw them. It was a raiding party. They beat their hands over their mouths, whooping. We had some rifles at Santa Irene, but all they were good for was making noise and turning the Indians even more savage.'

La Cautiva spoke like someone saying a prayer she had learned by heart, but out in the street I heard the desert Indians and their war cries. There was an eruption and, as if riding in on horseback in the fragments of some dream, they were in the room. They were local toughs and they were drunk. Now, in my memory, I see them as very tall. The one who came in at the head of them elbowed past Rufino, who stood by the door. Rufino changed colour and got out of the way. The lady in black, who had not stirred from her place, rose to her feet.

'It's Juan Moreira!' she said.

After so much time, I no longer know whether I remember the man of that night – the outlaw Moreira – or somebody else I was later often to see around cattle fairs. The long, thick hair and black beard of stage characters based on Moreira come to mind, but I also recall a ruddy face pitted by smallpox. The little dog scurried forward to give him a welcome. With a single whiplash, Moreira left it in a sprawl on the floor. It lay on its back and died pawing the air. This is where my story really begins.

Without a sound I made my way to one of the doors, which opened into a narrow passageway and a staircase. On the upper floor, I hid myself in a dark room. Apart from the bed, which was very low, I never knew what other furniture was there. I was trembling. Below, the shouting did not let up, and there was a shattering of glass. I heard a woman's footsteps coming up the stairs and I saw a momentary slit of light. Then La Cautiva's voice called out to me in a whisper. 'I'm here to serve – but to serve peaceable people,' she said. 'Come closer, I'm not going to hurt you.'

She had taken off her dressing gown. I lay beside her and felt for her face with my hands. I have no idea how much time passed. We exchanged neither a word nor a kiss. I untied her braid, and my hands played with her hair, which was very straight, and then they played with her. We did not see each other again after that, and I never learned her real name.

A shot startled us. La Cautiva said, 'You can leave by the other stairway.'

I did, and I found myself out in the dirt alley. It was a moonlit night. A police sergeant, Andrés Chirino, stood on watch by the wall with a rifle and fixed bayonet. He laughed, saying to me, 'I see you're an early riser.'

I must have answered something, but he paid me no attention. A man was lowering himself over the wall. With a bound, the sergeant buried the steel in his flesh. The man dropped to the ground, where he lay on his back, moaning and bleeding to death. I remembered the dog. To finish the man off once and for all, Chirino sank the bayonet in again.

'You didn't make it this time, Moreira,' he said almost joyously.

From every side came uniformed men, who had surrounded the house, and then the neighbours. The sergeant had a struggle to pull out the bayonet. Everybody wanted to shake his hand.

'The fancy footwork's all over for this hoodlum,' Rufino said with a laugh.

I went from group to group, telling people what I had seen. Then, all at once, I felt very tired; maybe I was even feverish. Slipping away, I found Rufino and we started home. From our horses, we saw the pale dawn light. More than tired, I felt dazed by that torrent of events.

'By the great river of that night,' my father said when the man had finished.

'That's right,' he agreed. 'In the bare space of a few hours I had known love and had looked on death. All things are revealed to all men – or, anyway, all those things it's granted a man to know – but to me two fundamental things were revealed in a single night. The years pass and I've told this story so many times I no longer know whether I remember it as it was or whether it's only my words I'm remembering. Maybe the same thing happened to La Cautiva with her Indian raid. It doesn't matter now whether it was I or someone else who saw Moreira killed.'

The mirror and the mask

The battle of Clontarf over, in which the Norwegians met defeat, the High King of Ireland spoke to his court poet. 'The greatest deeds lose their lustre if they are not coined in words,' the king said. 'I want you to sing my victory and my praise. I will be Aeneas; you will be my Virgil. Do you think yourself capable of this task, which will make us both immortal?'

'Yes, my lord,' said the bard. 'I am Ollan. For twelve winters I have trained in the disciplines of prosody. I know by heart the three hundred and sixty legends that form the basis of true poetry. The cycles of Ulster and Munster are in the strings of my harp. The laws authorize me to be lavish in using the oldest words of our tongue and the most complex metaphors. I have mastered the secret of writing, which protects our art from the undiscerning eyes of the common herd. I can celebrate loves, cattle thieves, voyages, and wars. I know the mythological lineages of all the royal houses of Ireland. I possess a knowledge of judicial astrology, mathematics, canon law, and the powers of plants. I have defeated my rivals in public contest. I have made myself skilled in satire, which causes infirmities of the skin, including leprosy. I know how to wield a sword, as I proved in your battle. I am ignorant of only one thing – how to thank you for the gift you make me.'

The king, who was easily tired by long speeches, especially those of others, said with relief, 'I know these things quite well. I have been told that the nightingale recently sang in England. When the rains and snows pass, and the nightingale returns from its southern lands, you will sing your praises before the court and before the School of Bards. I grant you a whole year. You will polish each word and letter. Reward, as you know by now, will not be unworthy of my royal custom nor of the sleepless nights of your inspiration.'

'O king, what greater reward than to see your face!' said the poet, who was also a courtier. He bowed and withdrew, already glimpsing one or two verses.

When the year came round – it had been a time of epidemics and uprisings – the poet presented his panegyric. He declaimed it slowly, confidently, without a glance at the manuscript. With his head the king showed his approval. Everyone imitated his gesture, even those thronging the doorways, who were unable to make out a single word. At the end the king spoke.

'I accept your labour,' he said. 'It is another victory. You have given each word its true meaning, and each substantive the epithet given it by the poets of old. In your whole panegyric there is not a single image unknown to the classics. War is the beautiful web of men, and blood is the sword's water. The sea has its gods and the clouds foretell the future. You have skilfully handled rhyme, alliteration, assonance, quantities, the artifices of learned rhetoric, the wise variation of metres. If all the literature of Ireland were to perish – absit omen – it could be reconstructed without loss from your classic ode. Thirty scribes shall copy it twelve times each.'

There was a silence, then he went on. 'All is well and yet nothing has happened. In our veins the blood runs no faster. Our hands have not sought the bow. No one has turned pale. No one uttered a battle cry or set his breast against the Vikings. Before a year is out, poet, we shall applaud another ode. As a sign of our approval, take this mirror, which is of silver.'

'I give thanks and I understand,' said the bard.

The stars in the sky went on in their bright course. Once more the nightingale sang in the Saxon forests, and the poet came back with his manuscript, which was shorter than the one before. He did not repeat it from memory but read it, obviously hesitant, omitting certain passages as if he himself did not completely understand them or did not wish to profane them. The ode was strange. It was not a description of the battle – it was the battle. In its warlike chaos there struggled with one another the God that is Three and is One, Ireland's pagan deities, and those who would wage war hundreds of years later at the beginning of the Elder Edda. The form was no less odd. A singular noun governed a plural verb. The prepositions were alien to common usage. Harshness alternated with sweetness. The metaphors were arbitrary, or so they seemed.

The king exchanged a few words with the men of letters who stood around him, then spoke to the bard. 'Your first ode I could declare was an apt compendium of all that has been sung in Ireland,' the king said. 'This one outdoes, and even makes as nothing, whatever came before it. It astounds, it dazzles, it causes wonderment. The ignorant will be unworthy of it, but not so the learned, the few. An ivory casket will be the resting place of its single copy. Of the pen that has produced so eminent a work we may expect one still more lofty.' He added with a smile, 'We are the figures of a fable, and it is good to remember that in fables the number three prevails.'

'The wizard's three gifts, triads, and the unquestionable Trinity,' the bard made bold to murmur.

The king continued, 'As a token of our approval, take this golden mask.'

'I give thanks and I have understood,' said the bard.

55

The anniversary came round again. The palace sentries noticed that the poet carried no manuscript. In amazement, the king looked at him; the bard was like another man. Something other than time had furrowed and transformed his features. His eyes seemed to stare into the distance or to be blind. The bard begged to be allowed a few words with the king. The slaves left the chamber.

'Have you not written the ode?' asked the king.

'Yes,' the bard sadly replied. 'But would that Christ Our Lord had prevented me!'

'Can you repeat it?'

'I dare not.'

'I will give you the courage you lack,' said the king.

The bard recited the poem. It consisted of a single line.

Not venturing to repeat it aloud, the poet and his king savoured it as if it were a secret prayer or a blasphemy. The king was as awestricken and overcome as the bard. The two looked at each other, very pale.

'In my youth,' said the king, 'I sailed towards the sunset. On one island I saw silver hounds that dealt death to golden boars. On another we fed ourselves on the fragrance of magic apples. On a third I saw walls of fire. On the farthest island of all an arched and hanging river cut across the sky and in its waters went fishes and boats. These are wonders, but they do not compare with your poem, which in some way encompasses them all. What bewitchery gave it to you?'

'In the dawn I woke up speaking words I did not at first understand,' said the bard. 'Those words were a poem. I felt I had committed a sin, perhaps one the Holy Ghost does not forgive.'

'The one we two now share,' the king said in a whisper. 'The sin of having known Beauty, which is a gift forbidden to men. Now it behoves us to expiate it. I gave you a mirror and a golden mask; here is my third present, which will be the last.'

In the bard's right hand he placed a dagger.

Of the poet, we know that he killed himself upon leaving the palace; of the king, that he is a beggar wandering the length and breadth of Ireland – which was once his kingdom – and that he has never repeated the poem.

Undr

The reader should be forewarned that the following pages will not be found in the *Libellus* (1615) of Adam of Bremen, who, as everyone knows, was born and died in the eleventh century. They were unearthed by Lappenberg in a manuscript in the Bodleian, at Oxford, and, given the wealth of circumstantial details, he judged them a late interpolation, but he published them as a curiosity in his *Analecta Germanica* (Leipzig, 1894). The opinion of a mere Argentine amateur is of little account; let the reader judge these pages for himself. My translation is faithful, but it is not literal. Adam of Bremen wrote:

. . . Of the peoples who live on the edge of the wilderness that stretches away on the other shore of the Barbarian Gulf, beyond the lands where the wild horse breeds, the worthiest of mention are the Urns. The uncertain or invented information of traders, the dangers of the route, and the plundering of nomads prevented me from reaching their territory. It is clear, however, that their rudimentary, unfrequented villages are located in the lowlands of the Vistula. Unlike the Swedes, the Urns profess the true faith of Christ, untainted by Arianism or by the bloodthirsty worship of devils, from which the royal houses of England and other northern nations trace their lineages. The Urns are herdsmen, ferrymen, shamans, forgers of swords, and harness makers. Owing to the rigours of war, they barely till the soil. One invariably comes to resemble one's enemies, and the steppe and the tribes that roam it have made the Urns very skilled in the handling of horse and bow. Their spears, since they are used by horsemen and not foot soldiers, are longer than ours.

As may be imagined, the Urns are unfamiliar with pen, inkhorn, and parchment. They carve their characters as our ancestors carved the runes which Odin revealed to them after having hung from the ash tree – Odin given to Odin – through nine days and nights.

To this general information I add an account of what I was told by a traveller from Iceland, Ulf Sigurdsson, a man of grave and measured words. We met in Uppsala, near the temple. The wood fire had died, and the cold and the dawn entered through the uneven chinks in the wall. Outside, the grey wolves, which eat the flesh of the heathens sacrificed to the three gods, left their wary tracks in the snow. Our conversation began in Latin, as is usual with churchmen, but we were not long in slipping into the tongue of the north, which extends from Thule all the way to the marketplaces of Asia. The man said:

As I am of the race of the skalds, to learn that the poetry of the Urns consists of a single word was enough for me to set out in search of them and the way that would lead to their land. Not without exhaustion and hardship did I arrive there after a year-long journey. It was night, and all those I came upon shot me odd looks, and one or two stones were hurled at me.

Seeing the light of a blacksmith's forge, I approached it. The smith, whose name was Orm, offered me lodging for the night. His language was more or less ours. We exchanged a few words. From his lips I heard for the first time the name of the reigning king – Gunnlaug. I learned that after his last war he looked with suspicion upon strangers and that it was his custom to crucify them.

59

To avoid that fate, which is less fitting to a man than a god, I undertook the composition of a *drápa*, or ode, that celebrated the victories, the fame, and the mercy of the king. I had barely commited it to memory when two men came searching for me. I did not want to surrender my sword to them, but I let myself be led away.

There were still stars in the sky. We crossed the first of several stretches of open ground with huts on every side. I had been led to expect pyramids, but what I saw in the middle of this square was a yellow wooden post. At the top of it I made out the black figure of a fish. Orm, who had accompanied us, said that the fish was the Word. In the next opening, I saw a red post marked with a disk. Orm said that this was the Word. I asked him to tell me it. He was a simple artisan, he said, and he did not know. In the third opening, which was the last, I saw a post painted black, with a design on it that I have forgotten. On the far side of the square was a long, straight wall whose ends I could not catch sight of. Later I found out that it was circular, that it supported a mud roof, that it enclosed a single chamber, and that it stretched around the whole city.

The horses tied to the hitching post outside were of small stature and had long manes. The blacksmith was not allowed entrance. Inside there were armed men, all standing. Gunnlaug, the king, who was ailing, lay with his eyes half shut on some camel hides on a kind of dais. He was a wasted, yellowish man, a sacred and almost forgotten thing; old scars spanned the width of his chest. One of the soldiers opened a way for me. Someone had brought a harp. Kneeling, I intoned the *drápa* in a low voice. There was no lack of the rhetorical figures, the alliterations, and the stresses that the form demands. I do not know whether the king understood it, but he gave me a silver ring, which I still preserve. Under his pillow, I glimpsed the edge of a dagger. To his right was a chessboard with a hundred squares and a handful of scattered pieces.

The guard shoved me to the rear. A man took my place before the king but did not kneel. He plucked the harp as if tuning it, and in a low voice he uttered the word that I had come in search of and had not yet fathomed.

'It no longer means anything now,' someone said reverently.

I saw tears. The man raised or modulated his voice, and his scarcely varying chords were monotonous or, still better, infinite. I would have liked his song to go on forever and to be my life. Abruptly, it stopped. I heard the noise the harp made when the singer, no doubt in utter exhaustion, threw it down. We all went out in disorder. I was one of the last. In astonishment I saw that the light was waning on another day. I walked a few steps, when a hand on my shoulder made me pause.

'The king's ring was your talisman,' I was told, 'but you will not be long in meeting your death, because you have heard the Word. I, Bjarni Thorkelsson, will save you. I am of the race of the skalds. In your ode you called blood the sword's water and a battle the web of men. I remember having heard those figures from my father's father. You and I are poets, and I will save you. Nowadays, we do not define each thing that our song quickens; we express it in a single word, which is the Word.'

'I was unable to hear it,' I said. 'I beg you to tell me what it is.'

He paused for a moment or two and replied, 'I have sworn not to divulge it. Besides, nobody can teach anything. You must find it out for yourself. But let's hurry; your life is in danger. I'll hide you in my house, where no one will dare look for you. If the wind is favourable, tomorrow you will sail southward on the river.'

So began the adventure that was to last so many winters.

61

I shall not go into all that befell me, nor shall I try to give an orderly account of my shifting fortunes. I was an oarsman, slave dealer, slave, woodcutter, highwayman, singer, and taster of deep waters and metals. I suffered captivity, and spent a year in the quicksilver mines, which loosen one's teeth. I fought side by side with men of Sweden in the Varangian guard at Mikligarðr [Constantinople]. On the shores of the Sea of Azov I was loved by a woman whom I shall never forget; I left her or she left me – it amounts to the same thing. I betrayed and I was betrayed. More than once fate made me kill. A Greek soldier challenged me and gave me the choice between two swords. One was a hand's breadth longer than the other. Knowing he was out to intimidate me, I chose the shorter. He asked me why. I replied that with either the distance from my hand to his heart was the same. At the edge of the Black Sea stands the runic epitaph I carved for my comrade in arms, Leif Arnarson. I have fought the Blue Men of Serkland, the Saracens. In the course of time I have been many men; it was a whirlwind, a long dream, but all the while the main thing was the Word. From time to time I disbelieved in it. I kept telling myself that to renounce the beautiful game of combining beautiful words was senseless, and that there was no reason to search for a single, and perhaps imaginary, word. Such reasoning was vain. A missionary suggested the word 'God', which I rejected. One early dawn, along the banks of a river that widened into a sea, I believed I had come upon the revelation.

Returning to the land of the Urns, I had some trouble finding the singer's house. When I did, I entered and spoke my name. By that time, night had fallen. From the floor, Thorkelsson told me to light a candle in the bronze candlestick. His face had aged so much that I could not help thinking that I, too, was old. As is the custom, I asked about his king.

'The king is no longer called Gunnlaug,' he said. 'His name is now another. Tell me all about your travels.'

I did so in exact order and with a great many details that I shall omit here. Before I had finished, he asked me, 'Did you often sing in those lands?'

The question took me by surprise. 'At first, I sang to earn my living,' I said. 'Later, overcome by a fear I do not understand, I was estranged from my harp and my song.'

'All right,' he said. 'You may go on with your story now.'

I obeyed. After I had finished, a long silence followed.

'The first woman you had – what did she give you?' he asked.

'Everything,' I said.

'Life gave me everything as well. Life gives everything to everyone, but most men are unaware of it. My voice is tired and my fingers weak, but listen to me.'

He took up his harp and uttered the word '*undr*', which means 'wonder'. The dying man's song held me rapt, but in it and in his chords I recognized my own verses, the slave woman who gave me my first love, the men I had killed, the chill of dawn, daybreak over the water, the oars. I took up the harp and sang to a different word.

'All right,' the other man said, and I had to draw close to hear him. 'You have understood.'

Utopia of a tired man

He called it *Utopia*, a Greek word meaning *there is no such place*.

– Quevedo

No two hills are alike, but everywhere on earth plains are one and the same. I was making my way in such country, asking myself, not that it really mattered, if this were Oklahoma or Texas or the part of the Argentine that literary men called the pampa. Neither to right nor left did I see a fence. As on other occasions, I slowly repeated these lines by the poet Emilio Oribe:

> At the heart of the endless awesome plain
> and close by the border of Brazil.

which keep growing and ever expanding.

The road was uneven. Rain began to fall. Some two or three hundred yards off I saw light from a house, which was low and rectangular and surrounded by trees. The door was opened by a man so tall he almost gave me a fright. He was dressed in grey. I felt he was waiting for someone. There was no lock on the door.

We went into a long room with wooden walls, a table, and chairs. A lamp giving off a yellowish light hung from the ceiling. The table, for some reason, seemed strange to me. On it stood an hourglass, the first, outside of some steel engraving or other, I had ever laid eyes on. The man motioned me to one of the chairs.

I tried out various languages, and we did not understand each other. When at last he spoke, he did so in Latin. I dusted off what I remembered from my now distant school days, readying myself for conversation.

'By your clothes, I see you come from another century,' he said. 'A diversity of tongues favoured a diversity of peoples and even of wars. The world has fallen back on Latin. There are those who fear it may degenerate again into French, Lemosi, or Papiamento, but that is not an immediate risk. Be that as it may, neither the past nor the future interests me.'

I said nothing, and he added, 'If you don't mind watching somebody else eat, will you join me?'

Seeing that he noticed my uneasiness, I said yes. We went down a corridor, with doors on either hand, that led to a small kitchen in which everything was made of metal. We came back with our dinner on a tray – bowls of cornflakes, a bunch of grapes, an unfamiliar fruit whose taste reminded me of figs, and a big pitcher of water. If I remember correctly, there was no bread. My host's features were sharp, and there was something unusual about his eyes. I won't forget his pale, austere face, which I shall never see again. He made no gestures when he spoke. Having to converse in Latin inhibited me, but at last I said, 'Doesn't my sudden appearance amaze you?'

'No,' he said. 'We receive such visits from century to century. They don't last long. Tomorrow, at the latest, you'll be home again.'

The certainty in his voice was reassuring. I thought it proper to introduce myself. 'I am Eudoro Acevedo. I was born in 1897, in the city of Buenos Aires. I am seventy years old. I am a professor of English and American literatures and a writer of imaginative tales.'

'I remember having read, not without pleasure, two tales of an imaginative nature,' he said. 'Travels of a Captain Lemuel Gulliver, which many people take to be true, and the *Summa Theologiae*. But let's not speak of facts. Facts matter to no one any more. They are mere points of departure for invention and reasoning. In our schools we are taught doubt and the art of forgetting – above all, the forgetting of what is personal and local. We live in time, which is successive, but we try to live sub specie aeternitatis. Of the past we retain a few names, which language tends to lose. We shun pointless details. We have neither dates nor history. Nor have we statistics. You said your name is Eudoro. I can't tell you my name, because I'm simply called Someone.'

'And what was your father's name?'

'He had none.'

On one of the walls I saw a shelf. I opened a book at random; the letters were clean and undecipherable, and they were written by hand. Their angular lines reminded me of the runic alphabet, which, however, was only used for writing inscriptions. I reflected that these men of the future were not only taller but were more skilled. Instinctively, I looked at the man's long, fine fingers.

'Now you are going to see something you've never seen,' he said. He handed me a copy of Thomas More's *Utopia*, printed in Basel in the year 1518; leaves and pages were missing.

Somewhat foolishly, I answered, 'It's a printed book. At home, I had over two thousand of them, though they were neither as old nor as valuable as this one.' I read the title aloud.

The man laughed. 'No one can read two thousand books. In the four centuries I have lived, I haven't read more than half a dozen. Besides, rereading, not reading, is what counts. Printing – which is now abolished, since it tended to multiply unnecessary texts to the point of dizziness – was one of man's worst evils.'

'In my strange past,' I said, 'the superstition prevailed that every day, between evening and morning, certain acts occur which it is a shame to be ignorant of. The planet was populated by collective ghosts – Canada, Brazil, the Swiss Congo, and the Common Market. Almost no one knew anything of the history that preceded those platonic entities, but, of course, they knew every last detail of the most recent congress of pedagogues, or of imminent breakdowns in diplomatic relations, or of statements issued by presidents, drawn up by the secretary of a secretary and containing all the carefully worded haziness appropriate to the genre. These things were read to be forgotten, for, only hours later, other trivialities would blot them out. Of all offices, that of politician was without doubt the most public. An ambassador or a Cabinet minister was a kind of cripple whom it was necessary to cart around in long, noisy vehicles, ringed by motorcyclists and military escorts and awaited by eager photographers. It seems that their feet have been cut off, my mother used to say. Pictures and the printed word were more real than the things they stood for. Only what was published had any reality. *Esse est percipi* (to be is to be photographed) was the beginning, middle, and end of our singular idea of the world. In that past of mine, people were naïve; they believed that certain merchandise was good because its own makers claimed so over and over again. Robberies were also frequent, though everyone knew that the possession of money brings no greater happiness or peace of mind.'

'Money?' the man echoed. 'No one any longer suffers poverty, which must have been unbearable, or wealth, which must have been the most uncomfortable form of vulgarity. Everyone has a calling.'

'Like the rabbis,' I said.

He appeared not to understand and went on. 'Nor are there cities anymore. To judge by the ruins of Bahía Blanca, which I once explored, not much has been lost. There are no personal possessions now, there are no inheritances. At the age of a hundred, when a man matures, he is ready to come face to face with himself and his lone-liness. By then he will have fathered a child.'

'One child?' I asked.

'Yes. Only one. There is no reason to carry on the human race. Some people think man is an organ of the godhead for universal consciousness, but nobody knows for sure whether such a godhead exists. The advantages and disadvantages of gradual or simultaneous suicide by every man and woman on earth are, I believe, now being argued. But let's get back to what we were saying.'

I agreed.

'Having reached a hundred, the individual no longer stands in need of love or friendship. Evils and involuntary death are no threat to him. He practises one of the arts or philosophy or mathematics or he plays a game of solitary chess. When he wants to, he kills himself. Man is master of his life. He is also master of his death.'

'Is that a quotation?' I asked.

'Of course. Quotations are all we have now. Language is a system of quotations.'

'And the great adventure of my time – space travel?' I asked.

'It's centuries ago now that those travels were given up. They were certainly to be admired, but we could never rid ourselves of a here and now.' With a smile, he added, 'Besides, all travel is spatial. To go from one planet to another is like going to the farm across the way. When you entered this room, you were carrying out a voyage through space.'

'That's right,' I said. 'And one also used to speak of chemical substances and animals.'

The man now turned his back to me and looked outside. Beyond the windows, the plain was white with silent snow and moonlight.

I got up my courage to ask, 'Are there still museums and libraries?'

'No. We try to forget the past, except for the writing of elegies. There are no commemorations or anniversaries or effigies of dead men now. Each of us must himself produce the arts and sciences he needs.'

'Then everyone must be his own Bernard Shaw, his own Jesus Christ, his own Archimedes.'

He agreed without a word.

'What happened to governments?'

'According to tradition, they fell into gradual disuse,' he said. 'They called elections, declared wars, collected taxes, confiscated fortunes, ordered arrests, and tried to impose censorship, but nobody on earth obeyed them. The press stopped publishing the news and photographs of government leaders. Politicians had to find honest work; some of them made good comedians or good faith healers. What actually happened was probably far more complex than this summary.' He went on in a changed tone. 'I built this house, which is the same as all others. I carved this furniture and these utensils. I worked these fields, which will be improved by people unknown to me. May I show you a few things?'

I followed him into an adjoining room. He lit a lamp like the first one; it too, hung from the ceiling. In a corner I saw a harp with few strings. On the walls were rectangular canvases in which yellow tones predominated. The work did not seem that of the same hand.

'This is what I do,' he said.

I examined the canvases, stopping before the smallest one, which represented, or suggested, a sunset and which encompassed something infinite.

'If you like it, you can have it as a keepsake of a future friend,' he said matter-of-factly.

I thanked him, but there were a few canvases that left me uneasy. I won't say that they were blank, but they were nearly so.

'They're painted in colours that your eyes of the past can't see,' he said.

A moment later, when his delicate hands plucked the strings of the harp, I barely caught an occasional sound. Just then a knock was heard.

A tall woman and three or four men entered the house. One would have said that they were brothers and sisters or that time had made them alike. My host spoke to the woman first.

'I knew you wouldn't fail to come tonight. Have you seen Nils?'

'Off and on. He's as devoted to his painting as ever.'

'Let's hope with more success than his father.'

The dismantling began. Manuscripts, pictures, furnishings, utensils – we left nothing in the house. The woman worked alongside the men. I was ashamed of my weakness, which scarcely allowed me to be of any help. No one shut the door and we went out, loaded with things. I noticed that the house had a saddle roof.

After a fifteen-minute walk, we turned left. In the distance I made out a kind of tower, crowned with a cupola.

'It's the crematory,' someone said. 'Inside it is the lethal chamber. It's said to have been invented by a philanthropist whose name, I think, was Adolf Hitler.'

The caretaker, whose stature by now did not astonish me, opened the gate to us. My host exchanged a few words with him. Before stepping into the enclosure, he waved goodbye.

'It looks like more snow,' the woman said.

In my study on Mexico Street, in Buenos Aires, I have the canvas that someone will paint, thousands of years from now, with substances today scattered over the whole planet.

The bribe

My story is about two men or, rather, about an episode involving two men. The actual affair, in itself neither singular nor even out of the ordinary, matters less than the character of its protagonists. Each of them sinned out of vanity, but in different ways and with different results. The events giving rise to the anecdote (for really it is not much more) took place a short time ago. To my mind, it could only have happened where it did – in America.

I had occasion at the University of Texas, in Austin, to speak at length to one of the two, Dr Ezra Winthrop. This was towards the end of 1961. Winthrop was a professor of Old English (he did not approve of the term 'Anglo-Saxon', which to him suggested an artifact made of two parts). I can remember that without once contradicting me he corrected my many mistakes and rash assumptions about the language. I was told that in his examinations he never asked a single question but invited his students to expatiate upon this or that topic, leaving the choice up to them. Of old Puritan stock, a native of Boston, Winthrop had found it hard getting used to the habits and prejudices of the South. He missed the snow, but it is my observation that Northerners are conditioned to the cold, much as we Argentines are to the heat. I still preserve the image, now dim, of a rather tall man with grey hair, less agile than strong. Clearer is my memory of his colleague, Herbert Locke, who gave me a copy of

71

his book *Towards a History of the Kenning*, in which one reads that the Saxons were not long in dispensing with those somewhat too mechanical metaphors ('whale's road' for 'the sea', 'falcon of battle' for 'the eagle'), whereas the skalds went on combining and interweaving them to the point of inextricability. I mention Herbert Locke because he is an integral part of my story.

I now come to the Icelander, Eric Einarsson, who is perhaps the true protagonist. I never set eyes on him. He arrived in Texas in 1969, when I was in Cambridge, but the letters of a mutual friend, Ramón Martínez López, have left me feeling I know Einarsson intimately. I know that he was impetuous, energetic, and cold, and that in a land of tall men he was tall. Given his red hair, it was inevitable that his students dub him Eric the Red. In his opinion, the use of slang by a foreigner was forced and mistaken, making him an intruder, so he never condescended even to an occasional 'okay'. A serious scholar of the Nordic languages, of English, of Latin, and – although he would not admit it – of German, he found no difficulty in making his way in American universities.

Einarsson's first work of any consequence was a study of the four articles that De Quincey wrote on the Danish origins of Cumbrian dialect. This was followed by a study of one of the rural dialects of Yorkshire. Both publications were well received, but Einarsson felt his career needed a boost. In 1970, the Yale University Press published his lengthy critical edition of the Battle of Maldon. The scholarship of Einarsson's notes was undeniable; in the introduction, however, certain of his hypotheses stirred up controversy in the almost secret circles of academics. There he stated, for example, that in style the poem has an affinity – even if a remote one – with the heroic Finnsburh fragment and not with the deliberate rhetoric of Beowulf, and that its handling of moving circumstantial details strangely foreshadows the methods which, not unjustly, we admire in the Icelandic sagas. He also emended a number of readings in Elphinston's text. Einarsson was made full professor at Texas the same year he arrived.

As everyone knows, scholarly conferences are popular in American universities. Dr Winthrop, in his turn, had given a paper at one of the important Germanic symposia the year before, at Michigan State. His department head, who was getting ready to go off on sabbatical, asked Winthrop to choose a delegate to deliver a paper at the next conference, to be held at Wisconsin. There were only two real candidates – Herbert Locke and Eric Einarsson.

Winthrop, like Carlyle, had renounced the Puritan faith of his ancestors but not its ethics. His duty was clear, and he did not decline to give his advice. Herbert Locke, going back to 1954, had been unstinting in his assistance to him, particularly with regard to a certain annotated edition of Beowulf which, in a number of universities, had replaced Klaeber's edition. Locke was now compiling a very useful work for the Germanic specialist – an English–Anglo-Saxon dictionary that would save readers from the often useless examination of etymological dictionaries. The Icelander was considerably younger; his insolence had earned him everyone's dislike, including Winthrop's. Einarsson's critical edition of Maldon had contributed a good deal to spreading his name. He was a master of polemic, and at the symposium he would cut a better figure than the shy, taciturn Locke.

Winthrop was in the midst of these considerations when there appeared in the review columns of the *Yale Philological Quarterly* a long article on the teaching of Anglo-Saxon. The piece was signed with the giveaway initials 'E. E.' and, as if to allay any doubt, under them it read 'University of Texas'. Written in a foreigner's correct English, the article, while not admitting of the least in-

73

civility, embodied a certain violence. It argued that to begin Anglo-Saxon by studying Beowulf, the work of an early period but in a pseudo-Virgilian, rhetorical style, was as arbitrary as to begin the study of English with the elaborate poetry of Milton. Its author advised an inversion of chronological order, starting, say, with the eleventh-century poem 'The Grave', in which the everyday language comes through, and then going back to the origins. As for Beowulf, some excerpt from its tedious aggregate of over three thousand lines was enough – for example, the funeral rites of Scyld, who came from the sea and returns to the sea. There was no mention of Winthrop's name in the article, but nonetheless he felt himself stiffly attacked. This mattered less to him, however, than the fact that his teaching method had been impugned.

Only a few days were left. Wanting to be fair, Winthrop could not allow Einarsson's article, which was being widely commented upon, to influence his decision. The choice between Locke and the Icelander gave him no small trouble. Winthrop spoke to Lee Rosenthal, the department chairman, one morning, and that same afternoon Einarsson was officially named to make the trip to Wisconsin.

On the eve of his departure, Einarsson presented himself in Ezra Winthrop's office. He had come to say goodbye and to thank Winthrop. One of the windows opened onto a tree-lined side street, and the two men were surrounded by shelves of books. Einarsson was quick to recognize a first edition of the *Edda Islandorum*, bound in parchment. Winthrop told him that he was sure Einarsson would do a good job and that he had nothing to thank him for. Their conversation, if I am not mistaken, was long.

'Let's speak frankly,' said Einarsson. 'Everyone knows that in honouring me with representing the university, Rosenthal is acting upon your advice. I am a good Germanic scholar; I'll do my best not to disappoint him.

The tongue of my childhood is the tongue of the sagas, and I pronounce Anglo-Saxon better than my British colleagues. My students say "*cyning*", not "*cunning*". They also know that smoking is absolutely forbidden in my classes and that they cannot come to them rigged out as hippies. As regards my unsuccessful rival, it would be in very bad taste were I to criticize him. In his book on the kenning he demonstrates not only his research into original sources but also into the pertinent works of Meissner and Marquardt. But let's put all this nonsense aside. I owe you a personal explanation.'

Einarsson paused, gave a glance out the window, and resumed. 'I left my country at the end of 1964,' he said. 'When someone decides to emigrate to a distant land, he fatally imposes upon himself the duty of getting on in that land. My first two small works, whose nature was strictly philological, had no other object than to demonstrate my ability. That, obviously, was not enough. I had always been interested in the Battle of Maldon, which I can repeat from memory – with an occasional slip or two. I managed to get Yale to publish my critical edition of it. The poem records a Norse victory, as you know, but as regards the notion that it may have influenced the later Icelandic sagas, I judge that inadmissible and absurd. I hinted at this merely to flatter English-speaking readers.'

The Icelander held Winthrop in his gaze. 'I come now to the heart of the matter – my polemical piece in the *Quarterly*. As you are aware, it justifies, or tries to justify, my system, but it deliberately exaggerates the drawbacks of yours, which, in exchange for imposing on the student the boredom of three thousand consecutive lines of intricate verse that narrate a confused story, endows him with a large vocabulary, allowing him to enjoy – if by then he has not given it up – the entire corpus of Anglo-Saxon literature. To go to Wisconsin was my real aim. You and

I, my dear friend, know that these conferences are foolish and that they entail pointless expense but that they can prove useful in one's career.'

Winthrop looked at him in surprise. The New Englander was an intelligent man, but he tended to take things seriously – including conferences and the world, which may very well be a cosmic joke.

'You perhaps remember our first conversation,' Einarsson went on. 'I had arrived from New York. It was a Sunday. The university dining halls were closed, and we had lunch at the Nighthawk. I learned a great deal from that meeting. As a good European, I had always supposed that the American Civil War was a crusade against slave owners; you argued that the South was within its rights to wish to secede from the Union and to maintain its own institutions. To lend greater strength to what you were saying, you told me that you were a Northerner and that one of your forebears had fought in that war in the ranks of Henry Halleck. You also praised the courage of the Confederates. I have an unusual flair for making instant assessments. That morning was enough for me. I realized, my dear Winthrop, that you are governed by the curious American passion for impartiality. You want, above all, to be fair-minded. Precisely because you are a Northerner, you attempt to understand and justify the South's cause. As soon as I knew that my trip to Wisconsin depended on what you might say to Rosenthal, I pressed the *Quarterly* to get my article into print, knowing that to criticize your teaching methods was the best means of getting your vote.'

There was a long silence. Winthrop was the first to break it. 'I'm an old friend of Herbert's, whose work I esteem,' he said. 'Directly or indirectly, you attacked me. To have denied you my vote would have been a sort of reprisal. I assessed his merits and yours, and the result you already know.' He added, as if thinking aloud,

'Maybe I gave in to the vanity of not seeking revenge. As you see, your stratagem worked.'

'Stratagem is the right word,' Einarsson replied, 'but I do not regret what I did. I shall always act in the best interests of our department. Be that as it may, I was determined to go to Wisconsin.'

'My first Viking,' said Winthrop, looking Einarsson straight in the eye.

'Another romantic superstition. It is not enough to be a Scandinavian to have descended from Vikings. My forefathers were good pastors of the Evangelical church; at the beginning of the tenth century, my ancestors may have been good priests of Thor. In my family, as far as I know, there were never any seafarers.'

'There were many in mine,' Winthrop said. 'Still, we aren't so different. One sin is common to us both – vanity. You pay me this visit to boast of your clever stratagem; I backed you to boast that I am an upright man.'

'Another thing is common to us,' said Einarsson. 'Nationality. I am an American citizen. My destiny is here, not in Ultima Thule. You would say that a passport does not change a man's nature.'

Then, shaking hands, they took leave of each other.

Avelino Arredondo

The event took place in Montevideo in 1897.

Every Saturday, in the way of the honest poor who
know they cannot invite people home or else are trying
to escape home, a group of young men occupied the
same side table at the Café del Globo. They were all
from Montevideo, and they had found it hard at first to
make friends with Arredondo, a man from the interior,
who neither confided in others nor encouraged others to
confide in him. A little over twenty years old, he was lean
and dark, rather short, and maybe a bit clumsy. His would
have been an almost anonymous face had his eyes – at
one and the same time sleepy and lively – not rescued it. He
worked as a clerk in a drygoods store on Buenos Aires
Street, studying law in his spare time. When the others con-
demned the war that ravaged the country and that, according to general opinion, the president was prolonging for
unworthy reasons, Arredondo remained silent. He also remained silent when they made fun of him for being stingy.

A short while after the battle of Cerros Blancos, Arredondo told his companions that they would not be seeing
him for a time, since he had to travel to Mercedes. The
news stirred no one. Somebody told him to watch out
for the gaucho rabble of Aparicio Saravia, the rebel
leader of the Whites. With a smile, Arredondo answered
that he was not afraid of the Whites. The other man,
who was a White himself, said nothing.

His goodbye to Clara, his fiancée, Arredondo found harder. He made it in almost the same words he had used with his friends, warning her not to expect letters, as he would be very busy. Clara, who was not in the habit of writing, accepted the explanation without a protest. The two were very much in love.

Arredondo lived on the outskirts of town. He was looked after by a mulatto woman who bore the same surname as he, since her forebears had been slaves of his family many years earlier, at the time of the Great War. Clementina was completely trustworthy, and he ordered her to tell anyone who came looking for him that he was away in the country. He had already collected his last pay from the drygoods store.

He moved into a back room of his house – one that opened onto the earth-paved third patio. It was a pointless measure, but it helped him to initiate his self-imposed reclusion. From the narrow iron bed, in which he was beginning to take naps again, he looked with a touch of melancholy at a bare shelf. He had sold his books – even his textbooks. All he had left was a Bible that he had never read before and that he would never finish reading.

He leafed through it page by page – sometimes out of interest, sometimes out of boredom – and he took upon himself the task of learning by heart some chapter or other of Exodus and the end of Ecclesiastes. He made no effort to understand what he read. He was a freethinker, but he never let a single night pass without saying the Lord's Prayer, which, on coming to Montevideo, he had promised his mother he would do. To fail in this filial promise, he thought, might bring him bad luck.

Arredondo knew that his goal was the morning of the twenty-fifth of August. He knew the exact number of days he had to get through. Once his goal was attained, time would cease, or, rather, nothing that happened after that would matter. He awaited the date like someone awaiting a boon or a liberation. He had let his clock run down so as not to be forever looking at it, but every night, on hearing the twelve dark strokes of midnight on a town clock, he tore a leaf out of the calendar and thought, *One day less*.

In the beginning he worked to build up a routine – brewing maté, smoking Turkish cigarettes that he rolled himself, reading and rereading a set number of pages, trying to converse with Clementina when she brought him his meals on a tray, and, before putting out the candle, repeating and embellishing the speech he planned to give. Talking to Clementina, a woman well along in years, was not at all easy, for her memory had remained rooted in the countryside and in its daily life. Arredondo also laid out a chessboard, on which he played haphazard games that never came to a conclusion. He was missing a rook, which he replaced with a bullet or with a two-cent coin.

To fill time, he cleaned his room every morning, chasing away spiders with a dustcloth and broom. The mulatto woman did not like his doing these menial tasks, which were her domain and which, in addition, he was not especially good at. He would have preferred waking with the sun already high, but his habit of getting up at dawn was stronger than his will. He missed his friends a good deal but, without feeling bitter about it, he knew that, given his invincible reserve, they were not missing him. One evening, one of them came to ask for him and was turned away from the door. Clementina did not know the caller, and Arredondo never learned who it was. He had been an avid reader of newspapers, and now he found it hard giving up these museums of ephemeral tidbits. He was not a man cut out for deep thinking or for deliberating.

His days and his nights were all the same, but Sundays weighed most on him. Towards the middle of July, he suspected that it had been a mistake to parcel out time, which in some way bears us along. Presently, he let his imagination wander over the length and breadth of Uruguay, then running with blood – over the rolling fields of Santa Irene, where he had flown kites; over a certain pinto, which by now would be dead; over the dust raised by cattle when they are herded by drovers; over the weary stagecoach that came from Fray Bentos once a month with its hoard of trinkets; over the bay of La Agraciada, where the Thirty-Three, the country's national heroes, had disembarked; over the Hervidero; over the hill ranges, the woods, and the rivers; over the Cerro, where he had climbed up to the lighthouse, thinking that on either bank of the Plate there was no other hill like it. From this hill overlooking the bay of Montevideo his thoughts passed on to the hill of the Uruguayan national emblem, and he fell asleep.

Every night the breeze off the sea brought a coolness propitious to sleep. He was never wakeful. He loved his fiancée completely, but it had been said that a man should not think about women – above all when they are not there. Life in the country had accustomed him to chastity. As for this other business, he tried to think as little as possible about the man he hated. The din of the rain on the flat roof kept him company.

To a man in jail or to a blind man, time flows downstream, as if along an easy slope. Halfway through his reclusion, Arredondo experienced more than once that almost timeless time. In the first of the house's three patios there was a cistern with a frog in it. It never occurred to Arredondo to think that the frog's time, which borders on eternity, was what he himself sought.

When the date was not far off, his impatience began again. One night, unable to bear it any longer, he went out into the street. Everything seemed different, larger. Turning a corner, he saw a light and entered a saloon. To justify his presence, he ordered a bitter rum. Some soldiers, leaning on the wooden bar, were holding forth.

'You know it's absolutely forbidden to give out news of battles,' one of them said. 'Listen to what happened yesterday evening. This will amuse you. A few of us were passing by *La Razón*, when we heard a voice inside defying the order. Losing no time, we marched in. The office was pitch-dark, but we riddled with bullets whoever was doing the talking. We wanted to drag him out by the heels. When it was quiet, we searched the place for him, but what we found was one of those machines they call a phonograph, which speaks by itself.'

All of them laughed. 'What do you think of a dodge like that, farmer?' the soldier said to Arredondo, who had been eavesdropping. Arredondo kept silent.

The uniformed man brought his face close to Arredondo's and said, 'Quick! Let me hear you shout, "Long live the president of our country – Juan Idiarte Borda!"'

Arredondo did not disobey, and amid mocking applause he managed to reach the door. He was in the street when a final insult was hurled at him. 'Fear's no fool,' he heard. 'It kills anger.' Arredondo had behaved like a coward, but he knew he was not one. Slowly he made his way back home.

On the twenty-fifth of August, Avelino Arredondo woke up at a little after nine. He thought first of Clara and only later of the date. 'Goodbye to waiting,' he told himself then, relieved. 'Today's the day.'

He shaved without hurrying, and in the mirror he found his everyday face. He chose a red necktie and put on his best clothes. He ate a late lunch. The overcast sky threatened drizzle. He had always imagined the sky would be bright and blue. A touch of sadness came over him as he left his damp room for the last time. In the arched entranceway he met Clementina and gave her his few remaining pesos. On the sign over the hardware store he saw the coloured diamond shapes, meaning paint was sold there, and he reflected that for over two months he had not given them a thought. He walked towards Sarandí Street. It was a holiday and very few people were about.

The clock had not struck three when he reached the Plaza Matriz. The 'Te Deum' was already over. A group of dignitaries – government officials, Army officers, and prelates – was coming down the slow steps of the church. At first sight, the tall hats – some still in hand – the uniforms, the gold braid, the arms, and the tunics created the illusion that the group was large; in reality, there were no more than about thirty people. Arredondo, who felt no fear, was filled with a kind of respect. He asked someone which was the president.

'You see the archbishop, with his mitre and crosier – the one beside him,' he was told.

Arredondo drew a revolver and opened fire. Idiarte Borda took one or two steps, fell headlong, and said distinctly, 'I've been shot!'

Arredondo gave himself up to the authorities. Later he was to declare, 'I am a Colorado, a Red, and I say it with pride. I've killed the president, who betrayed and tainted our party. I broke with my friends and my fiancée, so as not to implicate them. I did not look at the newspapers, so that nobody could say they had incited me. I claim this act of justice as my own. Now – let me be judged.'

This is the way it probably happened, although in a more involved fashion; this is the way I imagine it happened.

The disk

I am a woodcutter. My name does not matter. The hut where I was born and where I shall probably soon die stands at the edge of the forest.

It is said of the forest that it stretches as far as the sea, which rings the whole earth and on which wooden huts like mine wend their way. Never having seen this sea, I don't know. Nor have I ever seen the other side of the forest. When we were boys my elder brother made me vow that between us we would chop down the entire woods until not a single tree was left. My brother died, and what I seek now – and what I shall go on seeking – is something else. To the west runs a stream that I know how to fish with my hands. In the forest there are wolves, but wolves do not scare me, and my axe has never been untrue to me.

Of my years I have never kept count. I know they are many. My eyes no longer see. In the village, where I venture no more, since I would lose my way, I am known as a miser. But how much treasure can a mere woodcutter have laid up?

To keep snow out, I shut tight the door of my house with a stone. One evening long ago, I heard laboured foot-steps approach, and then a knock. I opened, and a stranger came in. He was old and tall, and he was wrapped in a threadbare blanket. A scar marked his face. His years seemed to have given him more authority than frailty, but I noticed that he was unable to get about without the aid of a staff. We exchanged a few words that I no longer remember. At the end, he said, 'I am homeless and sleep wherever I can. I have travelled the length and breadth of this land of the Saxons.'

These words testified to his years. My father had always spoken of the Saxon land, which nowadays people call England.

I had bread and fish. We did not speak a word during the meal. Rain began to fall. With a few skins I made him a pallet on the earth floor, where my brother had died. When night fell, we went to sleep.

Day was dawning when we left the hut. The rain had stopped and the ground was covered with new-fallen snow. My companion's staff slipped from his hand and he ordered me to pick it up.

'Why must I obey you?' I asked him.

'Because I am a king,' he answered.

I thought him mad. Picking up the staff, I handed it to him. He spoke with a different voice.

'I am king of the Secgens,' he said. 'Often in hard-pitched battle I carried my people to victory, but at the fateful hour I lost my kingdom. My name is Isern and I am of the race of Odin.'

'I do not worship Odin,' I said. 'I worship Christ.'

He went on as if he had not heard me. 'I travel the paths of exile, but I am still king, for I have the disk. Do you want to see it?'

He opened the palm of his bony hand. There was nothing in it. Only then did I recall that he had always kept the hand closed.

Staring hard at me, he said, 'You may touch it.'

With a certain misgiving, I touched my fingertips to his palm. I felt something cold, and saw a glitter. The hand closed abruptly. I said nothing. The man went on patiently, as if speaking to a child.

85

'It is Odin's disk,' he said, 'It has only one side. In all the world there is nothing else with only one side. As long as the disk remains mine, I shall be king.'

'Is it golden?' I said.

'I don't know. It is Odin's disk and it has only one side.'

Then and there I was overcome with greed to own the disk. If it were mine, I could trade it for an ingot of gold and I would be a king. I said to the vagabond, whom to this day I go on hating, 'In my hut I have buried a box of coins. They are of gold and they shine like an axe. If you give me Odin's disk, I'll trade you the box.'

He said stubbornly, 'I don't want to.'

'Then,' I said, 'you may continue on your path.'

He turned his back to me. One blow with the axe at the back of his neck was more than enough to bring him down, but as he fell his hand opened, and in the air I saw the glitter. I took care to mark the spot with my axe, and dragged the dead man to the stream, which was running high. There I threw him in.

Coming back to my hut, I searched for the disk. I did not find it. That was years ago, and I am searching still.

The Book of Sand

Thy rope of sands . . . – George Herbert

The line is made up of an infinite number of points; the plane of an infinite number of lines; the volume of an infinite number of planes; the hypervolume of an infinite number of volumes . . . No, unquestionably this is not – *more geometrico* – the best way of beginning my story. To claim that it is true is nowadays the convention of every made-up story. Mine, however, *is* true.

I live alone in a fourth-floor apartment on Belgrano Street, in Buenos Aires. Late one evening, a few months back, I heard a knock at my door. I opened it and a stranger stood there. He was a tall man, with nondescript features – or perhaps it was my myopia that made them seem that way. Dressed in grey and carrying a grey suitcase in his hand, he had an unassuming look about him. I saw at once that he was a foreigner. At first, he struck me as old; only later did I realize that I had been misled by his thin blond hair, which was, in a Scandinavian sort of way, almost white. During the course of our conversation, which was not to last an hour, I found out that he came from the Orkneys.

I invited him in, pointing to a chair. He paused awhile before speaking. A kind of gloom emanated from him – as it does now from me.

'I sell Bibles,' he said.

Somewhat pedantically, I replied, 'In this house are several English Bibles, including the first – John Wiclif's.

87

I also have Cipriano de Valera's, Luther's – which, from a literary viewpoint, is the worst – and a Latin copy of the Vulgate. As you see, it's not exactly Bibles I stand in need of.'

After a few moments of silence, he said, 'I don't only sell Bibles. I can show you a holy book I came across on the outskirts of Bikaner. It may interest you.'

He opened the suitcase and laid the book on a table. It was an octavo volume, bound in cloth. There was no doubt that it had passed through many hands. Examining it, I was surprised by its unusual weight. On the spine were the words 'Holy Writ' and, below them, 'Bombay'.

'Nineteenth-century, probably,' I remarked.

'I don't know,' he said. 'I've never found out.'

I opened the book at random. The script was strange to me. The pages, which were worn and typographically poor, were laid out in double columns, as in a Bible. The text was closely printed, and it was ordered in versicles. In the upper corners of the pages were Arabic numbers. I noticed that one left-hand page bore the number (let us say) 40,514 and the facing right-hand page 999. I turned the leaf; it was numbered with eight digits. It also bore a small illustration, like the kind used in dictionaries – an anchor drawn with pen and ink, as if by a schoolboy's clumsy hand.

It was at this point that the stranger said, 'Look at the illustration closely. You'll never see it again.'

I noted my place and closed the book. At once, I reopened it. Page by page, in vain, I looked for the illustration of the anchor. 'It seems to be a version of Scriptures in some Indian language, is it not?' I said to hide my dismay.

'No,' he replied. Then, as if confiding a secret, he lowered his voice. 'I acquired the book in a town out on the plain in exchange for a handful of rupees and a Bible. Its owner did not know how to read. I suspect that he saw the Book of Books as a talisman. He was of the lowest caste; nobody but other untouchables could tread his shadow without contamination. He told me his book was called the Book of Sand, because neither the book nor the sand has any beginning or end.'

The stranger asked me to find the first page.

I laid my left hand on the cover and, trying to put my thumb on the flyleaf, I opened the book. It was useless. Every time I tried, a number of pages came between the cover and my thumb. It was as if they kept growing from the book.

'Now find the last page.'

Again I failed. In a voice that was not mine, I barely managed to stammer, 'This can't be.'

Still speaking in a low voice, the stranger said, 'It can't be, but it *is*. The number of pages in this book is no more or less than infinite. None is the first page, none the last. I don't know why they're numbered in this arbitrary way. Perhaps to suggest that the terms of an infinite series admit any number.'

Then, as if he were thinking aloud, he said, 'If space is infinite, we may be at any point in space. If time is infinite, we may be at any point in time.'

His speculations irritated me. 'You are religious, no doubt?' I asked him.

'Yes, I'm a Presbyterian. My conscience is clear. I am reasonably sure of not having cheated the native when I gave him the Word of God in exchange for his devilish book.'

I assured him that he had nothing to reproach himself for, and I asked if he were just passing through this part of the world. He replied that he planned to return to his country in a few days. It was then that I learned that he was a Scot from the Orkney Islands. I told him I had a great personal affection for Scotland, through my love of Stevenson and Hume.

'You mean Stevenson and Robbie Burns,' he corrected.

While we spoke, I kept exploring the infinite book. With feigned indifference, I asked, 'Do you intend to offer this curiosity to the British Museum?'

'No. I'm offering it to you,' he said, and he stipulated a rather high sum for the book.

I answered, in all truthfulness, that such a sum was out of my reach, and I began thinking. After a minute or two, I came up with a scheme.

'I propose a swap,' I said. 'You got this book for a handful of rupees and a copy of the Bible. I'll offer you the amount of my pension cheque, which I've just collected, and my black-letter Wiclif Bible. I inherited it from my ancestors.'

'A black-letter Wiclif!' he murmured.

I went to my bedroom and brought him the money and the book. He turned the leaves and studied the title page with all the fervour of a true bibliophile.

'It's a deal,' he said.

It amazed me that he did not haggle. Only later was I to realize that he had entered my house with his mind made up to sell the book. Without counting the money, he put it away.

We talked about India, about Orkney, and about the Norwegian jarls who once ruled it. It was night when the man left. I have not seen him again, nor do I know his name.

I thought of keeping the Book of Sand in the space left on the shelf by the Wiclif, but in the end I decided to hide it behind the volumes of a broken set of The Thousand and One Nights. I went to bed and did not sleep. At three or four in the morning, I turned on the light. I got down the impossible book and leafed through its pages. On one of them I saw engraved a mask. The upper corner of the page carried a number, which I no longer recall, elevated to the ninth power.

I showed no one my treasure. To the luck of owning it was added the fear of having it stolen, and then the misgiving that it might not truly be infinite. These twin preoccupations intensified my old misanthropy. I had only a few friends left; I now stopped seeing even them. A prisoner of the book, I almost never went out anymore. After studying its frayed spine and covers with a magnifying glass, I rejected the possibility of a contrivance of any sort. The small illustrations, I verified, came two thousand pages apart. I set about listing them alphabetically in a notebook, which I was not long in filling up. Never once was an illustration repeated. At night, in the meagre intervals my insomnia granted, I dreamed of the book.

Summer came and went, and I realized that the book was monstrous. What good did it do me to think that I, who looked upon the volume with my eyes, who held it in my hands, was any less monstrous? I felt that the book was a nightmarish object, an obscene thing that affronted and tainted reality itself.

I thought of fire, but I feared that the burning of an infinite book might likewise prove infinite and suffocate the planet with smoke. Somewhere I recalled reading that the best place to hide a leaf is in a forest. Before retirement, I worked on Mexico Street, at the Argentine National Library, which contains nine hundred thousand volumes. I knew that to the right of the entrance a curved staircase leads down into the basement, where books and maps and periodicals are kept. One day I went there and, slipping past a member of the staff and trying not to notice at what height or distance from the door, I lost the Book of Sand on one of the basement's musty shelves.

Afterword

Prefacing stories a reader has not yet read, since it demands the analysis of plots that it may be inconvenient to deal with in advance, is a somewhat impossible task. I therefore prefer an afterword.

The book's first story takes up the old theme of the double, which several times moved Robert Louis Stevenson's ever-fortunate pen. In England, its name is 'fetch' or, more bookishly, 'wraith of the living'; in Germany, '*Doppelgänger*'. One of its earliest names, I suspect, was 'alter ego'. This ghostly apparition probably came from mirrors of metal or from reflections in water or simply from memory, which makes of anyone both a spectator and an actor. In 'The Other', I had to ensure that the speakers were sufficiently different to be two persons and alike enough to be one. Is it worth stating that the idea for the story came to me in Cambridge on the banks of the Charles River, whose cold course reminded me of the far-off course of the Rhone?

The theme of love is quite common in my poems but not in my prose, which offers no other example than 'Ulrike'. The reader will notice its formal affinity with 'The Other'.

'The Congress' is perhaps the most ambitious of the tales in this book; its subject is that of an enterprise so vast that in the end it becomes confused with the world itself and with the sum of daily life. Its opaque beginning tries to imitate that of a Kafka story; its end tries, doubtless in vain, to match the ecstasies of Chesterton and John Bunyan. I have never been worthy of such a revelation, but I managed to dream one up. I have woven into the story – as is my habit – a number of autobiographical elements.

Life, which everyone knows is inscrutable, left me no peace until I perpetrated a posthumous story by H. P. Lovecraft, a writer whom I have always considered an unconscious parodist of Poe. In the end, I gave in; the lamentable fruit is entitled 'There Are More Things'.

'The Sect of the Thirty' salvages, without a shred of documentation, the tale of a possible heresy.

'The Night of the Gifts' is perhaps the most innocent, most violent, and most exalted story offered by this collection.

An earlier story of mine, 'The Library of Babel' (1941), imagines an infinite number of books; 'Undr' and 'The Mirror and the Mask', centuries-old literatures that are made up of a single line or word.

'Utopia of a Tired Man' is in my judgement the most honest and melancholy piece in the collection.

I have always been amazed by the ethical obsession of Americans. 'The Bribe' attempts to reflect this trait.

In spite of John Felton, Charlotte Corday, the well-known opinion of Rivera Indarte ('It is a holy act to kill Rosas'), and the Uruguayan National Anthem ('If they are tyrants, Brutus' dagger'), I do not approve of political assassination. Be that as it may, readers of Avelino Arredondo's solitary crime might wish to know the story's outcome. The historian Luis Melián Lafinur asked for Arredondo's pardon, but his judges Carlos Fein and Cristóbal Salvanach sentenced him to a month in solitary confinement and five years' imprisonment. One of the streets of Montevideo now bears Arredondo's name.

Two opposite and inconceivable concepts are the subjects

of the last two stories. 'The Disk' is about the Euclidean circle, which has only one side; 'The Book of Sand', a volume of incalculable pages.

I hope that these hasty notes I have just dictated do not exhaust this book and that its dreams go on branching out in the hospitable imagination of those who now close it.

Buenos Aires, 3 February 1975   J. L. B.

The Gold of the Tigers

Selected later poems translated by Alastair Reid

Preface to *The Gold of the Tigers*

For anyone who has lived out seventy years, according to the Book of David, there is little to hope for except to go on plying familiar skills, with an occasional mild variation and with tedious repetitions. To escape, or possibly to extenuate, that monotony, I chose to admit, perhaps with rash hospitality, the miscellaneous interests that crossed my everyday writer's attention. Parable follows on the heels of confession, free or blank verse on the sonnet. In the earliest times, which were so susceptible to vague speculation and the inevitable ordering of the universe, there can have existed no division between the poetic and the prosaic. Everything must have been tinged with magic. Thor was not the god of thunder; he was the thunder and the god.

For a true poet, every moment of existence, every act, ought to be poetic since, in essence, it is so. As far as I know, no one to this day has attained that high state of awareness. Browning and Blake got closer to it than anyone else. Whitman aimed in that direction, but his careful enumerations do not always rise above a kind of crude cataloguing.

I distrust literary schools, which I judge to be didactic constructs designed to simplify what they preach; but if I were obliged to name the influence behind my poems, I would say they stemmed from *modernismo* – that enormous liberation that gave new life to the many literatures that use the Castilian language, and that certainly carried as far as Spain. I have spoken more than once with Leopoldo Lugones – that solitary, proud man – and he would interrupt the flow of the conversation to mention 'my friend and master, Rubén Darío'. (I think, furthermore, that we ought to emphasize the affinities within our language, and not its regional differences.)

My reader will notice, in some pages, a philosophical preoccupation. It has been with me since my childhood, when my father showed me, with the help of a chessboard (it was, I remember, a cedarwood board), the paradox of the race between Achilles and the tortoise.

As for the influences that show up in this volume ... First, the writers I prefer – I have already mentioned Robert Browning; next, those I have read and whom I echo; then, those I have never read but who are in me. A language is a tradition, a way of grasping reality, not an arbitrary assemblage of symbols.

Buenos Aires, 1972   J. L. B.

Preface to *The Unending Rose*

The romantic notion of a Muse who inspires poets was advanced by classical writers; the classical idea of the poem as a function of the intelligence was put forward by a romantic, Poe, around 1846. The fact is paradoxical. Apart from isolated cases of oneiric inspiration – the shepherd's dream referred to by Bede, the famous dream of Coleridge – it is obvious that both doctrines are partially true, unless they correspond to distinct stages in the process. (For Muse, we must read what the Hebrews and Milton called Spirit, and what our own woeful mythology refers to as the Subconscious.) In my own case, the process is more or less unvarying. I begin with the glimpse of a form, a kind of remote island, which will eventually be a story or a poem. I see the end and I see the beginning, but not what is in between. That is gradually revealed to me, when the stars or chance are propitious. More than once, I have to retrace my steps by way of the shadows. I try to interfere as little as possible in the evolution of the work. I do not want it to be distorted by my opinions, which are the most trivial things about us. The notion of art as compromise is a simplification, for no one knows entirely what he is doing. A writer can conceive a fable, Kipling acknowledged, without grasping its moral. He must be true to his imagination, and not to the mere ephemeral circumstances of a supposed 'reality'.

Literature starts out from poetry and can take centuries to arrive at the possibility of prose. After four hundred years, the Anglo-Saxons left behind a poetry which was not just occasionally admirable and a prose which was scarcely explicit. The word must have been in the beginning a magic symbol, which the usury of time wore out. The mission of the poet should be to restore to the word, at least in a partial way, its primitive and now secret force. All verse should have two obligations: to communicate a precise instance and to touch us physically, as the presence of the sea does. I have here an example from Virgil:

sunt lacrymae rerum et mentem mortalia tangunt

One from Meredith:

Not till the fire is dying in the grate
Look we for any kinship with the stars

Or this alexandrine from Lugones, in which the Spanish is trying to return to the Latin:

El hombre numeroso de penas y de días.

Such verses move along their shifting path in the memory.

After so many – too many – years of practising literature, I do not profess any aesthetic. Why add to the natural limits which habit imposes on us those of some theory or other? Theories, like convictions of a political or religious nature, are nothing more than stimuli. They vary for every writer. Whitman was right to do away with rhyme; that negation would have been stupid in Victor Hugo's case.

Going over the proofs of this book, I notice with some distaste that blindness plays a mournful role, which it does not play in my life. Blindness is a confinement, but it is also a liberation, a solitude propitious to invention, a key and an algebra.

June, 1975   J. L. B.

Tankas

1

Alto en la cumbre
todo el jardín es luna,
luna de oro.
Más precioso es el roce
de tu boca en la sombra.

2

La voz del ave
que la penumbra esconde
ha enmudecido.
Andas por tu jardín.
Algo, lo sé, te falta.

3

La ajena copa,
la espada que fue espada
en otra mano,
la luna de la calle,
¿dime, acaso no bastan?

4

Bajo la luna
el tigre de oro y sombra
mira sus garras.
No sabe que en el alba
han destrozado un hombre.

Tankas

1

High on the summit,
the garden is all moonlight,
the moon is golden.
More precious is the contact
of your lips in the shadow.

2

The sound of a bird
which the twilight is hiding
has fallen silent.
You pace the garden.
I know that you miss something.

3

The curious goblet,
the sword which was a sword once
in another grasp,
the moonlight on the street –
tell me, are they not enough?

4

Underneath the moon,
tiger of gold and shadow
looks down at his claws,
unaware that in the dawn
they lacerated a man.

5

Triste la lluvia
que sobre el mármol cae,
triste ser tierra.
Triste no ser los días
del hombre, el sueño, el alba.

6

No haber caído,
como otros de mi sangre,
en la batalla.
Ser en la vana noche
él que cuenta las sílabas.

5

Wistful is the rain
falling upon the marble,
sad to become earth,
sad no longer to be part
of man, of dream, of morning.

6

Not to have fallen,
like others of my lineage,
cut down in battle.
To be in the fruitless night
he who counts the syllables.

Susana Bombal

Alta en la tarde, altiva y alabada,
cruza el casto jardín y está en la exacta
luz del instante irreversible y puro
que nos da este jardín y la alta imagen
silenciosa. La veo aquí y ahora,
pero también la veo en un antiguo
crepúsculo de Ur de los Caldeos
o descendiendo por las lentas gradas
de un templo, que es innumerable polvo
del planeta y que fue piedra y soberbia,
o descifrando el mágico alfabeto
de las estrellas de otras latitudes
o aspirando una rosa en Inglaterra.
Está donde haya música, en el leve
azul, en el hexámetro del griego,
en nuestras soledades que la buscan,
en el espejo de agua de la fuente,
en el mármol de tiempo, en una espada,
en la serenidad de una terraza
que divisa ponientes y jardines.

Y detrás de los mitos y las máscaras,
el alma, que está sola.

Susana Bombal

Tall in the evening, arrogant, aloof,
she crosses the chaste garden and is caught
in the shutter of that pure and fleeting instant
which gives to us this garden and this vision,
unspeaking, deep. I see her here and now,
but simultaneously I also see her
haunting an ancient, twilit Ur of the Chaldees
or coming slowly down the shallow steps,
a temple, which was once proud stone but now
has turned to an infinity of dust,
or winkling out the magic alphabet
locked in the stars of other latitudes,
or breathing in a rose's scent, in England.
She is where music is, and in the gentle
blue of the sky, in Greek hexameters,
and in our solitudes, which seek her out.
She is mirrored in the water of the fountain,
in time's memorial marble, in a sword,
in the serene air of a patio,
looking out on sunsets and on gardens.

And underneath the myths and the masks,
her soul, always alone.

Cosas

El volumen caído que los otros
ocultan en la hondura del estante
y que los días y las noches cubren
de lento polvo silencioso. El ancla
de sidón que los mares de Inglaterra
oprimen en su abismo ciego y blando.
El espejo que no repite a nadie
cuando la casa se ha quedado sola.
Las limaduras de uña que dejamos
a lo largo del tiempo y del espacio.
El polvo indescifrable que fue Shakespeare.
Las modificaciones de la nube.
La simétrica rosa momentánea
que el azar dio una vez a los ocultos
cristales del pueril calidoscopio.
Los remos de Argos, la primera nave.
Las pisadas de arena que la ola
soñolienta y fatal borra en la playa.
Los colores de Turner cuando apagan
las luces en la recta galería
y no resuena un paso en la alta noche.
El revés del prolijo mapamundi.
La tenue telaraña en la pirámide.
La piedra ciega y la curiosa mano.
El sueño que he tenido antes del alba
y que olvidé cuando clareaba el día.
El principio y el fin de la epopeya
de Finsburh, hoy unos contados versos
de hierro, no gastado por los siglos.
La letra inversa en el papel secante.
La tortuga en el fondo del aljibe.

Things

The fallen volume, hidden by the others
from sight in the recesses of the bookshelves,
and which the days and nights muffle over
with slow and noiseless dust. Also, the anchor
of Sidon, which the seas surrounding England
press down into its blind and soft abyss.
The mirror which shows nobody's reflection
after the house has long been left alone.
Fingernail filings which we leave behind
across the long expanse of time and space.
The indecipherable dust, once Shakespeare.
The changing figurations of a cloud.
The momentary but symmetric rose
which once, by chance, took substance in the shrouded
mirrors of a boy's kaleidoscope.
The oars of Argus, the original ship.
The sandy footprints which the fatal wave
as though asleep erases from the beach.
The colours of a Turner when the lights
are turned out in the narrow gallery
and not a footstep sounds in the deep night.
The other side of the dreary map of the world.
The tenuous spiderweb in the pyramid.
The sightless stone and the inquiring hand.
The dream I had in the approaching dawn
and later lost in the clearing of the day.
The ending and beginning of the epic
of Finsburh, today a few sparse verses
of iron, unwasted by the centuries.
The mirrored letter on the blotting paper.
The turtle in the bottom of the cistern.

Lo que no puede ser. El otro cuerno
del unicornio. El Ser que es Tres y es Uno.
El disco triangular. El inasible
instante en que la flecha del eleata,
inmóvil en el aire, da en el blanco.
La flor entre las páginas de Becquer.
El péndulo que el tiempo ha detenido.
El acero que Odín clavó en el árbol.
El texto de las no cortadas hojas.
El eco de los cascos de la carga
de Junín, que de algún eterno modo
no ha cesado y es parte de la trama.
La sombra de Sarmiento en las aceras.
La voz que oyó el pastor en la montaña.
La osamenta blanqueando en el desierto.
La bala que mató a Francisco Borges.
El otro lado del tapiz. Las cosas
que nadie mira, salvo el Dios de Berkeley.

And that which cannot be. The other horn
of the unicorn. The Being, Three in One.
The triangular disk. The imperceptible moment
in which the Eleatic arrow.
motionless in the air, reaches the mark.
The violet pressed between the leaves of Becquer.
The pendulum which time has stayed in place.
The weapon Odin buried in the tree.
The volume with its pages still unslit.
The echo of the hoofbeats at the charge
of Junin, which in some enduring mode
never has ceased, is part of the webbed scheme.
The shadow of Sarmiento on the sidewalks.
The voice heard by the shepherd on the mountain.
The skeleton bleaching white in the desert.
The bullet which shot dead Francisco Borges.
The other side of the tapestry. The things
which no one sees, except for Berkeley's God.

El amenazado

Es el amor. Tendré que ocultarme o que huir.

Crecen los muros de su cárcel, como en un sueño atroz. La hermosa máscara ha cambiado, pero como siempre es la única. ¿De qué me servirán mis talismanes: el ejercicio de las letras, la vaga erudición, el aprendizaje de las palabras que usó el áspero Norte para cantar sus mares y sus espadas, la serena amistad, las galerías de la Biblioteca, las cosas comunes, los hábitos, el joven amor de mi madre, la sombra militar de mis muertos, la noche intemporal, el sabor del sueño?

Estar contigo o no estar contigo es la medida de mi tiempo.

Ya el cántaro se quiebra sobre la fuente, ya el hombre se levanta a la voz del ave, ya se han oscurecido los que miran por las ventanas, pero la sombra no ha traído la paz.

Es, ya lo sé, el amor: la ansiedad y el alivio de oír tu voz. la espera y la memoria, el horror de vivir en lo sucesivo,

Es el amor con sus mitologías, con sus pequeñas magias inútiles.

Hay una esquina por la que no me atrevo a pasar.

Ya los ejércitos me cercan, las hordas.

(Esta habitación es irreal; ella no la ha visto.)

El nombre de una mujer me delata.

Me duele una mujer en todo el cuerpo.

The threatened one

It is love. I will have to hide or flee.

Its prison walls grow larger, as in a fearful dream. The alluring mask has changed, but as usual it is the only one. What use now are my talismans, my touchstones: the practice of literature, vague learning, an apprenticeship to the language used by the flinty Northland to sing of its seas and its swords, the serenity of friendship, the galleries of the Library, ordinary things, habits, the young love of my mother, the soldierly shadow cast by my dead ancestors, the timeless night, the flavour of sleep and dream?

Being with you or without you is how I measure my time.

Now the water jug shatters above the spring, now the man rises to the sound of birds, now those who look through the windows are indistinguishable, but the darkness has not brought peace.

It is love, I know it; the anxiety and relief at hearing your voice, the hope and the memory, the horror at living in succession.

It is love with its own mythology, its minor and pointless magic.

There is a street corner I do not dare to pass.

Now the armies surround me, the rabble.

(This room is unreal. She has not seen it.)

A woman's name has me in thrall.

A woman's being afflicts my whole body.

Tú

Un solo hombre ha nacido, un solo hombre ha muerto en
la tierra.
Afirmar lo contrario es mera estadística, es una adición
imposible.
No menos imposible que sumar el olor de la lluvia y el
sueño que antenoche soñaste.
Ese hombre es Ulises, Abel, Caín, el primer hombre que
ordenó las constalaciones, el hombre que erigió la primera
pirámide, el hombre que escribió los hexagramas del
Libro de los Cambios, el forjador que grabó runas en
la espada de Hengist, el arquero Einar Tamberskelver,
Luis de León, el librero que engendró a Samuel Johnson,
el jardinero de Voltaire, Darwin en la proa del *Beagle*,
un judío en la cámara letal, con el tiempo, tú y yo.
Un solo hombre ha muerto en Ilión, en el Metauro, en
Hastings, en Austerlitz, en Trafalgar, en Gettysburg.
Un solo hombre ha muerto en los hospitales, en barcos,
en la ardua soledad, en la alcoba del hábito y del amor.
Un solo hombre ha mirado la vasta aurora.
Un solo hombre ha sentido en el paladar la frescura del
agua, el sabor de las frutas y de la carne.
Hablo del único, del uno, del que siempre está solo.

You

In all the world, one man has been born, one man has
   died.
To insist otherwise is nothing more than statistics, an
   impossible extension.
No less impossible than bracketing the smell of rain with
   your dream of two nights ago.
That man is Ulysses, Abel, Cain, the first to make con-
   stellations of the stars, to build the first pyramid, the
   man who contrived the hexagrams of the Book of
   Changes, the smith who engraved runes on the sword of
   Hengist, Einar Tamberskelver the archer, Luis de León,
   the bookseller who fathered Samuel Johnson, Voltaire's
   gardener, Darwin aboard the *Beagle*, a Jew in the death
   chamber, and, in time, you and I.
One man alone has died at Troy, at Metaurus, at Hastings,
   at Austerlitz, at Trafalgar, at Gettysburg.
One man alone has died in hospitals, in boats, in painful
   solitude, in the rooms of habit and of love.
One man alone has looked on the enormity of dawn.
One man alone has felt on his tongue the fresh quenching
   of water, the flavour of fruit and of flesh.
I speak of the unique, the single man, he who is always
   alone.

Poema de la cantidad

Pienso en el parco cielo puritano
de solitarias y perdidas luces
que Emerson miraría tantas noches
desde la nieve y el rigor de Concord.
Aquí son demasiadas las estrellas.
El hombre es demasiado. Las innúmeras
generaciones de aves y de insectos,
del jaguar constelado y de la sierpe,
de ramas que se tejen y entretejen,
del café, de la arena y de las hojas
oprimen las mañanas y prodigan
su minucioso laberinto inútil.
Acaso cada hormiga que pisamos
es única ante Dios, que la precisa
para la ejecución de las puntuales
leyes que rigen Su curioso mundo.
Si así no fuera, el universo entero
sería un error y un oneroso caos.
Los espejos del ébano y del agua,
el espejo inventivo de los sueños,
los líquenes, los peces, las madréporas,
las filas de tortugas en el tiempo,
las luciérnagas de una sola tarde,
las dinastías de las araucarias,
las perfiladas letras de un volumen
que la noche no borra, son sin duda
no menos personales y enigmáticas
que yo, que las confundo. No me atrevo
a juzgar a la lepra o a Calígula.

Poem of quantity

I think of the stark and puritanical sky
with its remote and solitary stars
which Emerson so many nights would look at
from the snow-bound severity of Concord.
Here, the night sky overflows with stars.
Man is too numerous. Endless generations
of birds and insects, multiplying themselves,
of serpents and the spotted jaguar,
of growing branches, weaving, interweaving,
of grains of sand, of coffee and of leaves
descend on every day and recreate
their minuscule and useless labyrinth.
It may be every ant we trample on
is single before God, Who counts on it
for the unfolding of the measured laws
which regulate His curious universe.
The entire system, if it was not so,
would be an error and a weighty chaos.
Mirrors of water, mirrors of ebony,
the all-inventive mirror of our dreams,
lichens, fishes, and the riddled coral,
the clawmarks left by tortoises in time,
the fireflies of a single afternoon,
the dynasties of the Auraucarians,
the delicate shapes of letters in a volume
which night does not blot out, unquestionably
are no less personal and enigmatic
than I, who mix them up. I would not venture
to judge the lepers or Caligula.

El centinela

Entra la luz y me recuerdo; ahí está.

Empieza por decirme su nombre, que es (ya se entiende)
el mío.

Vuelvo a la esclavitud que ha durado más de siete veces
diez años.

Me impone su memoria.

Me impone las miserias de cada día, la condición humana.

Soy su viejo enfermero; me obliga a que le lave los pies.

Me acecha en los espejos, en la caoba, en los cristales de
las tiendas.

Una u otra mujer lo han rechazado y debo compartir su
congoja.

Me dicta ahora este poema, que no me gusta.

Me exige el nebuloso aprendizaje del terco anglosajón.

Me ha convertido al culto idolátrico de militares muertos,
con los que acaso no podría cambiar una sola palabra.

En el último tramo de la escalera siento que está a mi lado.

Está en mis pasos, en mi voz.

Minuciosamente lo odio.

Advierto con fruición que casi no ve.

Estoy en una celda circular y el infinito muro se estrecha.

Ninguno de los dos engaña al otro, pero los dos mentimos.

Nos conocemos demasiado, inseparable hermano.

Bebes el agua de mi copa y devoras mi pan.

La puerta del suicida está abierta, pero los teólogos afirman
que en la sombra ulterior del otro reino estaré yo,
esperándome.

The watcher

The light enters and I remember who I am; he is there.
He begins by telling me his name which (it should now be
  clear) is mine.
I revert to the servitude which has lasted more than seven
  times ten years.
He saddles me with his rememberings.
He saddles me with the miseries of every day, the human
  condition.
I am his old nurse; he requires me to wash his feet.
He spies on me in mirrors, in mahogany, in shop windows.
One or another woman has rejected him, and I must share
  his anguish.
He dictates to me now this poem, which I do not like.
He insists I apprentice myself tentatively to the stubborn
  Anglo-Saxon.
He has won me over to the hero worship of dead soldiers,
  people with whom I could scarcely exchange a single
  word.
On the last flight of stairs, I feel him at my side.
He is in my footsteps, in my voice.
Down to the last detail, I abhor him.
I am gratified to remark that he can hardly see.
I am in a circular cell and the infinite wall is closing in.
Neither of the two deceives the other, but we both lie.
We know each other too well, inseparable brother.
You drink the water from my cup and you wolf down my
  bread.
The door to suicide is open, but theologians assert that, in
  the subsequent shadows of the other kingdom, there will
  I be, waiting for myself.

Al idioma alemán

Mi destino es la lengua castellana,
el bronce de Francisco de Quevedo,
pero en la lenta noche caminada
me exaltan otras músicas más intimas.
Alguna me fue dada por la sangre –
oh voz de Shakespeare y de la Escritura –,
otras por el azar, que es dadivoso,
pero a ti, dulce lengua de Alemania,
te he elegido y buscado, solitario.
A través de vigilias y gramáticas,
de la jungla de las declinaciones,
del diccionario, que no acierta nunca
con el matiz preciso, fui acercándome.
Mis noches están llenas de Virgilio,
dije una vez; también pude haber dicho
de Hölderlin y de Angelus Silesius.
Heine me dio sus altos ruiseñores;
Goethe, la suerte de un amor tardío,
a la vez indulgente y mercenario;
Keller, la rosa que una mano deja
en la mano de un muerto que la amaba
y que nunca sabrá si es blanca o roja.
Tú, lengua de Alemania, eres tu obra
capital: el amor entrelazado
de las voces compuestas, las vocales
abiertas, los sonidos que permiten
el estudioso hexámetro del griego
y tu rumor de selvas y de noches.
Te tuve alguna vez. Hoy, en la linde
de los años cansados, te diviso
lejana como el álgebra y la luna.

To the German language

My destiny is in the Spanish language,
the bronze words of Francisco de Quevedo,
but in the long, slow progress of the night,
different, more intimate musics move me.
Some have been handed down to me by blood –
voices of Shakespeare, language of the Scriptures –
others by chance, which has been generous;
but you, gentle language of Germany,
I chose you, and I sought you out alone.
By way of grammar books and patient study,
through the thick undergrowth of the declensions,
the dictionary, which never puts its thumb on
the precise nuance, I kept moving closer.
My nights were full of overtones of Virgil,
I once said; but I could as well have named
Hölderlin, Angelus Silesius.
Heine lent me his lofty nightingales;
Goethe, the good fortune of late love,
at the same time both greedy and indulgent;
Keller, the rose which one hand leaves behind
in the closed fist of a dead man who adored it,
who will never know if it is white or red.
German language, you are your masterpiece:
love interwound in all your compound voices
and open vowels, sounds which accommodate
the studious hexameters of Greek
and undercurrents of jungles and of nights.
Once, I had you. Now, at the far extreme
of weary years, I feel you have become
as out of reach as algebra and the moon.

Apenas lo entreveo y ya lo pierdo.
Ajustado el decente traje negro
y con una chalina como todas,
la frente angosta y el bigote ralo,
camina entre la gente de la tarde
ensimismado y sin mirar a nadie.
En una esquina de la calle Piedras
pide una caña brasilera. El hábito.
Alguien le grita adiós. No le contesta.
Hay en los ojos un rencor antiguo.
Otra cuadra. Una racha de milonga
le llega desde un patio. Esos changangos
están siempre amolando la paciencia,
pero al andar se hamaca y no lo sabe.
Sube la mano y palpa la firmeza
del puñal en la sisa del chaleco.
Va a cobrarse una deuda. Falta poco.
Unos pasos y el hombre se detiene.
En el zaguán hay una flor de cardo.
Oye el golpe del balde en el aljibe
y una voz que conoce demasiado.
Empuja la cancel que aún está abierta
como si lo esperaran. Esta noche
tal vez ya lo habrán muerto.

I catch a glimpse of him and then I lose him –
best black suit well-brushed and narrow-fitting,
nondescript neckerchief around the throat,
narrow forehead, straggling moustache,
he walks among the people of the evening,
lost in himself, not seeing anyone.
At a corner counter on the Calle Piedras
he takes a shot of spirits, out of habit.
Someone calls out to him. He doesn't answer.
Behind his eyes, an old resentment smoulders.
Another block. A fragment of milonga
falls from a patio. Those cheap guitars
keep gnawing at the edges of his temper,
but still, his walk keeps time, unconsciously.
He lifts his hand and pats the solid handle
of the dagger in the collar of his waistcoat.
He goes to reclaim a debt. It is not far.
A few steps, and the man stops in his walking.
In the passageway, there is a flowering thistle.
He hears the clunk of a bucket in the cistern
and a voice already too well-known to him.
He pushes the far door, which is already open
as though he were expected. This very evening
perhaps they will have shown him his own death.

Milonga de Manuel Flores

Manuel Flores va a morir.
Eso es moneda corriente;
morir es una costumbre
que sabe tener la gente.

Y sin embargo me duele
decircle adiós a la vida,
esa cosa tan de siempre,
tan dulce y tan conocida.

Miro en el alba mi mano,
miro en la mano las venas;
con extrañeza las miro
como si fueran ajenas.

Mañana vendrá la bala
y con la bala el olvido.
Lo dijo el sabio Merlín:
morir es haber nacido.

¡Cuánta cosa en su camino
Estos ojos habrán visto!
Quién sabe lo que verán
después que me juzgue Cristo.

Manuel Flores va a morir.
Eso es moneda corriente;
morir es una costumbre
que sabe tener la gente.

Milonga of Manuel Flores

Manuel Flores is doomed to die.
That's as sure as your money.
Dying is a custom
well-known to many.

But even so, it pains me
to say goodbye to living,
that state so well-known now,
so sweet, so solid-seeming.

I look at my hand in the dawning.
I look at the veins contained there.
I look at them in amazement
as I would look at a stranger.

Tomorrow comes the bullet,
oblivion descending.
Merlin the magus said it:
being born has an ending.

So much these eyes have seen,
such things, such places!
Who knows what they will see
when I've been judged by Jesus.

Manuel Flores is doomed to die.
That's as sure as your money.
Dying is a custom
well-known to many.

El sueño de Pedro Henríquez Ureña

El sueño que Pedro Henríquez Ureña tuvo en el alba de uno de los días de 1946 curiosamente no constaba de imágenes sino de pausadas palabras. La voz que las decía no era la suya pero se parecía a la suya. El tono, pese a las posibilidades patéticas que el tema permitía, era impersonal y común. Durante el sueño, que fue breve, Pedro sabía que estaba durmiendo en su cuarto y que su mujer estaba a su lado. En la obscuridad el sueño le dijo:

Hará unas cuantas noches, en una esquina de la calle Córdoba, discutiste con Borges la invocación del Anónimo Sevillano *Oh Muerte, ven callada como sueles venir en la saeta*. Sospecharon que era el eco deliberado de algún texto latino, ya que esas translaciones correspondían a los hábitos de una época, del todo ajena a nuestro concepto del plagio, sin duda menos literario que comercial. Lo que no sospecharon, lo que no podían sospechar, es que el diálogo era profético. Dentro de unas horas, te apresurarás por el último andén de Constitución, para dictar tu clase en la Universidad de La Plata. Alcanzarás el tren, pondrás la cartera en la red y te acomodarás en tu asiento, junto a la ventanilla. Alguien, cuyo nombre no sé pero cuya cara estoy viendo, te dirigirá unas palabras. No le contestarás, porque estarás muerto. Ya te habrás despedido como siempre de tu mujer y de tus hijas. No recordarás este sueño porque tu olvido es necesario para que se cumplan los hechos.

The dream of Pedro Henríquez Ureña

The dream which Pedro Henríquez Ureña dreamed close
to dawn one day in 1946 consisted, oddly enough, not of
images but of slow, specific words. The voice which spoke
them was not his own, but resembled it. Its tone, in spite
of the mournful possibilities implicit in what it said, was
impersonal and matter-of-fact. During the dream, which
was short, Pedro knew that he was asleep in his own
room, with his wife at his side. In the dark, the dream
addressed him:

Some nights ago, on a corner of the Calle Córboda, you
discussed with Borges the invocation of the Anonymous
One of Seville: 'O Death come in silence as you are wont
to do in the hands of the clock.' You both suspected it to
be the deliberate echo of some Latin text, inasmuch as
these transliterations corresponded with the habits of a
particular time, totally outside our own notions of plagiar-
ism, unquestionably less literary than practical. What you
did not suspect, what you could not suspect, is that the
dialogue was a prophetic one. In a few hours, you will be
hurrying along the last platform of Constitution Station,
to give your class at the University of La Plata. You will
catch the train, put your briefcase on the rack and settle
in your seat, beside the window. Someone, whose name
I do not know but whose face I am seeing, will address
some words to you. You will not reply, because you will
be dead. You will already have said goodbye, as usual,
to your wife and children. You will not remember this
dream, because your forgetting is necessary to the fulfil-
ment of these events.

El Palacio

El Palacio no es infinito.

Los muros, los terraplenes, los jardines, los laberintos, las gradas, las terrazas, los antepechos, las puertas, las galerías, los patios circulares o rectangulares, los claustros, las encrucijadas, los aljibes, las antecámaras, las cámaras, las alcobas, las bibliotecas, los desvanes, las cárceles, las celdas sin salida y los hipogeos, no son menos cuantiosos que los granos de arena del Ganges, pero su cifra tiene un fin. Desde las azoteas, hacia el poniente, no falta quien divise las herrerías, las carpinterías, las caballerizas, los astilleros y las chozas de los esclavos.

A nadie le está dado recorrer más que una parte infinitesimal del palacio. Alguno no conoce sino los sótanos. Podemos percibir unas caras, unas voces, unas palabras, pero lo que percibimos es ínfimo. Ínfimo y precioso a la vez. La fecha que el acero graba en la lápida y que los libros parroquiales registran es posterior a nuestra muerte; ya estamos muertos cuando nada nos toca, ni una palabra, ni un anhelo, ni una memoria. Yo sé que no estoy muerto.

The Palace

The Palace is not infinite.

The walls, the ramparts, the gardens, the labyrinths, the staircases, the terraces, the parapets, the doors, the galleries, the circular or rectangular patios, the cloisters, the intersections, the cisterns, the anterooms, the chambers, the alcoves, the libraries, the attics, the dungeons, the sealed cells and the vaults, are not less in quantity than the grains of sand in the Ganges, but their number has a limit. From the roofs, towards sunset, many people can make out the forges, the workshops, the stables, the boatyards and the huts of the slaves.

It is granted to no one to traverse more than an infinitesimal part of the palace. Some know only the cellars. We can take in some faces, some voices, some words, but what we perceive is of the feeblest. Feeble and precious at the same time. The date which the chisel engraves in the tablet, and which is recorded in the parochial registers, is later than our own death; we are already dead when nothing touches us, neither a word nor a yearning nor a memory. I know that I am not dead.

Hengist quiere hombres.

Acudirán de los confines de arena que se pierden en largos mares, de chozas llenas de humo, de tierras pobres de hondos bosques de lobos, en cuyo centro indefinido está el Mal.

Los labradores dejarán el arado y los pescadores las redes.

Dejarán sus mujeres y sus hijos, porque el hombre sabe que en cualquier lugar de la noche puede hallarlas y hacerlos.

Hengist el mercenario quiere hombres.

Los quiere para debelar una isla que todavía no se llama Inglaterra.

Le seguirán sumisos y crueles.

Saben que siempre fue el primero en la batalla de hombres.

Saben que una vez olvidó su deber de venganza y que le dieron una espada desnuda y que la espada hizo su obra.

Atravesarán a remo los mares, sin brújula y sin mástil.

Traerán espadas y broqueles, yelmos con la forma del jabalí, conjuros para que se multipliquen las mieses, vagas cosmogonías, fábulas de los hunos y de los godos.

Conquistarán la tierra, pero nunca entrarán en las ciudades que Roma abandonó, porque son cosas demasiado complejas para su mente bárbara.

Hengist los quiere para la victoria, para el saqueo, para la corrupción de la carne y para el olvido.

Hengist los quiere (pero no lo sabe) para la fundación

Hengist wants men.

They will rally from the edges of sand which dissolve into broad seas, from huts filled with smoke, from threadbare landscapes, from deep forests haunted by wolves, in whose vague centre Evil lurks.

The ploughmen will abandon the plough and the fishermen their nets.

They will leave their wives and their children, for a man knows that anywhere in the night he can encounter the one and engender the other.

Hengist the mercenary wants men.

He wants them to subdue an island which is not yet called England.

Cowed and vicious, they will follow him.

They know him always to have been the first among men in battle.

They know that once he forgot his vow of vengeance and that they gave him a naked sword and that the sword did its work.

They will try their oars against the seas, with neither compass nor mast.

They will bear swords and bucklers, helmets in the likeness of the boar's head, spells to make the cornfields multiply, vague cosmogonies, legends of the Huns and the Goths.

They will conquer the ground, but never will they enter the cities which Rome abandoned, for these are things too complicated for their primitive minds.

Hengist wants them for the victory, for the pillaging, for the corruption of the flesh and for oblivion.

Hengist wants them (but he does not know it) for the

del mayor imperio, para que canten Shakespeare y
Whitman, para que dominen el mar las naves de Nelson,
para que Adán y Eva se alejen, tomados de la mano y
silenciosos, del Paraíso que han perdido.
Hengist los quiere (pero no lo sabrá) para que yo trace
estas letras.

founding of the greatest of empires, for the singing of Shakespeare and Whitman, for Nelson's ships to rule the sea, for Adam and Eve to be banished, hand in hand and silent, from the Paradise they have lost.

Hengist wants them (but he cannot know it) so that I may form these letters.

A un gato

No son más silenciosos los espejos
ni más furtiva el alba aventurera;
eres, bajo la luna, esa pantera
que nos es dado divisar de lejos.
Por obra indescifrable de un decreto
divino, te buscamos vanamente;
más remoto que el Ganges y el poniente,
tuya es la soledad, tuyo el secreto.
Tu lomo condesciende a la morosa
caricia de mi mano. Has admitido,
desde esa eternidad que ya es olvido,
el amor de la mano recelosa.
En otro tiempo estás. Eres el dueño
de un ámbito cerrado como un sueño.

To a cat

Mirrors are not more wrapt in silences
nor the arriving dawn more secretive;
you, in the moonlight, are that panther figure
which we can only spy at from a distance.
By the mysterious functioning of some
divine decree, we seek you out in vain;
remoter than the Ganges or the sunset,
yours is the solitude, yours is the secret.
Your back allows the tentative caress
my hand extends. And you have condescended,
since that forever, now oblivion,
to take love from a flattering human hand.
You live in other time, lord of your realm –
a world as closed and separate as dream.

El oro de los tigres

Hasta la hora del ocaso amarillo
cuántas veces habré mirado
al poderoso tigre de Bengala
ir y venir por el predestinado camino
detrás de los barrotes de hierro,
sin sospechar que eran su cárcel.
Después vendrían otros tigres,
el tigre de fuego de Blake;
después vendrían otros oros,
el metal amoroso que era Zeus,
el anillo que cada nueve noches
engendra nueve anillos y éstos, nueve,
y no hay un fin.
Con los años fueron dejándome
los otros hermosos colores
y ahora sólo me quedan
la vaga luz, la inextricable sombra
y el oro del principio.
Oh ponientes, oh tigres, oh fulgores
del mito y de la épica,
oh un oro más precioso, tu cabello
que ansían estas manos.

The gold of the tigers

Up to the moment of the yellow sunset,
how many times will I have cast my eyes on
the sinewy-bodied tiger of Bengal
toing and froing on its paced-out path
behind the labyrinthine iron bars,
never suspecting them to be a prison.
Afterward, other tigers will appear:
the blazing tiger of Blake, burning bright;
and after that will come the other golds –
the amorous gold shower disguising Zeus,
the gold ring which, on every ninth night,
gives light to nine rings more, and these, nine more,
and there is never an end.
All the other overwhelming colours,
in company with the years, kept leaving me,
and now alone remains
the amorphous light, the inextricable shadow
and the gold of the beginning.
On sunsets, O tigers, O wonders
of myth and epic,
O gold more dear to me, gold of your hair
which these hands crave to touch.

Yo

La calavera, el corazón secreto,
los caminos de sangre que no veo,
los túneles del sueño, ese Proteo,
las vísceras, la nuca, el esqueleto.
Soy esas cosas. Increíblemente
soy también la memoria de una espada
y la de un solitario sol poniente
que se dispersa en oro, en sombra, en nada.
Soy él que ve las proas desde el puerto;
soy los contados libros, los contados
grabados por el tiempo fatigados;
soy él que envidia a los que ya se han muerto.
Más raro es ser el hombre que entrelaza
palabras en un cuarto de una casa.

The skull within, the secret, shuttered heart,
the byways of the blood I never see,
the underworld of dreaming, that Proteus,
the nape, the viscera, the skeleton.
I am all those things. Amazingly,
I am too the memory of a sword
and of a solitary, falling sun,
turning itself to gold, then grey, then nothing.
I am the one who sees the approaching ships
from harbour. And I am the dwindled books,
the rare engravings worn away by time;
the one who envies those already dead.
Stranger to be the man who interlaces
such words as these, in some room, in a house.

El sueño

Cuando los relojes de la media noche prodiguen
un tiempo generoso,
iré más lejos que los bogavantes de Ulises
a la región del sueño, inaccesible
a la memoria humana.
De esa región immersa rescato restos
que no acabo de comprender:
hierbas de sencilla botánica,
animales algo diversos,
diálogos con los muertos,
Rostros que realmente son máscaras,
palabras de lenguajes muy antiguos
y a veces un horror incomparable
al que nos puede dar el día.
Seré todos o nadie. Seré el otro
que sin saberlo soy, él que ha mirado
ese otro sueño, mi vigilia. La juzga,
resignado y sonriente.

The dream

While the clocks of the midnight hours are squandering
an abundance of time,
I shall go, farther than the shipmates of Ulysses,
to the territory of dream, beyond the reach
of human memory.
From that underwater world I save some fragments,
inexhaustible to my understanding:
grasses from some primitive botany,
animals of all kinds,
conversations with the dead,
faces which all the time are masks,
words out of very ancient languages,
and at times, horror, unlike anything
the day can offer us.
I shall be all or no one. I shall be the other
I am without knowing it, he who has looked on
that other dream, my waking state. He weighs it up,
resigned and smiling.

Browning resuelve ser poeta

Por estos rojos laberintos de Londres
descubro que he elegido
la más curiosa de las profesiones humanas,
salvo que todas, a su modo, lo son.
Como los alquimistas
que buscaron la piedra filosofal
en el azogue fugitivo,
haré que las comunes palabras —
naipes marcados del tahur, moneda de la plebe —
rindan la magia que fue suya
cuando Thor era el numen y el estrépito,
el trueno y la plegaria.
En el dialecto de hoy
diré a mi vez las cosas eternas;
trataré de no ser indigno
del gran eco de Byron.
Este polvo que soy será invulnerable.
Si una mujer comparte mi amor
mi verso rozará la décima esfera de los cielos
     concéntricos;
si una mujer desdeña mi amor
haré de mi tristeza una música,
un alto río que siga resonando en el tiempo.
Viviré de olvidarme.
Seré la cara que entreveo y que olvido,
seré Judas que acepta
la divina misión de ser traidor,
seré Calibán en la ciénaga,
seré un soldado mercenario que muere
sin temor y sin fe,
seré Polícrates que ve con espanto

Browning resolves to be a poet

In these red London labyrinths
I find that I have chosen
the most curious of human professions,
though given that all are curious, in their way.
Like alchemists
who looked for the philosopher's stone
in elusive quicksilver,
I shall make ordinary words –
the marked cards of the sharper, the people's coinage –
yield up the magic which was theirs
when Thor was inspiration and eruption,
thunder and worship.
In the wording of the day,
I in my turn will say eternal things;
I will try to be not unworthy
of the great echo of Byron.
This dust that is me will be invulnerable.
If a woman partakes of my love,
my poem will graze the tenth sphere of the concentric
  heavens;
if a woman shrugs off my love,
I will make music out of my misery,
a vast river reverberating on through time.
I will live by forgetting myself.
I will be the face I half-see and forget,
I will be Judas who accepts
the blessed destiny of being a traitor,
I will be Caliban in the swamp,
I will be a mercenary dying
without fear or faith,
I will be Polycrates, horrified to see

el anillo devuelto por el destino,
seré el amigo que me odia.
El persa me dará el ruiseñor y Roma la espada.
Máscaras, agonías, resurrecciones,
destejerán y tejerán mi suerte
y alguna vez seré Robert Browning.

the ring returned by destiny,
I will be the friend who hates me.
Persia will grant me the nightingale, Rome the sword.
Agonies, masks and resurrections
will weave and unweave my fate
and at some point I will be Robert Browning.

Inventario

Hay que arrimar una escalera para subir. Un tramo le falta.
¿Qué podemos buscar en el altillo
sino lo que amontona el desorden?
Hay olor a humedad.
El atardecer entra por la pieza de plancha.
Las vigas del cielo raso están cerca y el piso está vencido.
Nadie se atreve a poner el pie.
Hay un catre de tijera desvencijado.
Hay unas herramientas inútiles.
Está el sillón de ruedas del muerto.
Hay un pie de lámpara.
Hay una hamaca paraguaya con borlas, deshilachada.
Hay aparejos y papeles.
Hay una lámina del estado mayor de Aparicio Saravia.
Hay una vieja plancha a carbón.
Hay un reloj de tiempo detenido, con el péndulo roto.
Hay un marco desdorado, sin tela.
Hay un tablero de cartón y unas piezas descabaladas.
Hay un brasero de dos patas.
Hay una petaca de cuero.
Hay un ejemplar enmohecido del *Libro de los Mártires* de
   Foxe, en intrincada letra gótica.
Hay una fotografía que ya pueda ser de cualquiera.
Hay una piel gastada que fue de tigre.
Hay una llave que ha perdido su puerta.
¿Qué podemos buscar en el altillo
sino lo que amontona el desorden?
Al olvido, a las cosas del olvido, acabo de erigir este monu-
   mento
sin duda menos perdurable que el bronce y que se con-
   funde con ellas.

Inventory

To reach it, a ladder has to be set up. There is no stair.
What can we be looking for in the attic
but the accumulation of disorder?
There is a smell of damp.
The late afternoon enters by way of the laundry.
The ceiling beams loom close, and the floor has rotted.
Nobody dares to put a foot on it.
A folding cot, broken.
A few useless tools,
the dead one's wheelchair.
The base for a lamp.
A Paraguayan hammock with tassels, all frayed away.
Equipment and papers.
An engraving of Aparicio Saravia's general staff.
An old charcoal iron.
A clock stopped in time, with a broken pendulum.
A peeling gilt frame, with no canvas.
A cardboard chessboard, and some broken chessmen.
A stove with only two legs.
A chest made of leather.
A mildewed copy of Foxe's *Book of Martyrs*, in intricate
  Gothic lettering.
A photograph which might be of anybody.
A worn skin, once a tiger's.
A key which has lost its lock.
What can we be looking for in the attic
except the flotsam of disorder?
To forgetting, to all forgotten objects, I have just erected
  this monument
(unquestionably less durable than bronze) which will be
  lost among them.

El suicida

No quedará en la noche una estrella.
No quedará la noche.
Moriré y conmigo la suma
del intolerable universo.
Borraré las pirámides, las medallas,
los continentes y las caras.
Borraré la acumulación del pasado.
Haré polvo la historia, polvo el polvo.
Estoy mirando el último poniente.
Oigo el último pájaro.
Lego la nada a nadie.

The suicide

Not a single star will be left in the night.
The night will not be left.
I will die and, with me,
the weight of the intolerable universe.
I shall erase the pyramids, the medallions,
the continents and faces.
I shall erase the accumulated past.
I shall make dust of history, dust of dust.
Now I am looking on the final sunset.
I am hearing the last bird.
I bequeath nothingness to no one.

Al ruiseñor

¿En qué noche secreta de Inglaterra
o del constante Rhin incalculable,
perdida entre las noches de mis noches,
a mi ignorante oído habrá llegado
tu voz cargada de mitologías,
ruiseñor de Virgilio y de los persas?
Quizá nunca te oí, pero a mi vida
se une tu vida, inseparablemente.
Un espíritu errante fue tu símbolo
en un libro de enigmas. El Marino
te apodaba sirena de los bosques
y cantas en la noche de Julieta
y en la intrincada página latina
y desde los pinares de aquel otro
ruiseñor de Judea y de Alemania,
Heine el burlón, el encendido, el triste.
Keats te oyó para todos, para siempre.
No habrá uno solo entre los claros nombres
que los pueblos te dan sobre la tierra
que no quiera ser digno de tu música,
ruiseñor de la sombra. El agareno
te soñó arrebatado por el éxtasis
el pecho traspasado por la espina
de la cantada rosa que enrojeces
con tu sangre final. Asiduamente
urdo en la hueca tarde este ejercicio,
ruiseñor de la arena y de los mares,
que en la memoria, exaltación y fábula,
ardes de amor y mueres melodioso.

To the nightingale

Out of what secret English summer evening
or night on the incalculable Rhine,
lost among all the nights of my long night,
could it have come to my unknowing ear,
your song, encrusted with mythology,
nightingale of Virgil and the Persians?
Perhaps I never heard you, but my life
is bound up with your life, inseparably.
The symbol for you was a wandering spirit
in a book of enigmas. And among all sailors,
you were nicknamed 'siren of the woods';
you sing throughout the night of Juliet
and through the intricate pages of the Latin
and from the pinewoods of that other one,
the nightingale of Germany and Judea,
Heine, the clown, the man on fire, the sad one.
Keats heard your song for everyone, for ever.
There is not one among the shimmering names
people have given you across the earth
which does not seek to match your own music,
nightingale of the dark. The Muslim dreamed you
in the delirium of ecstasy,
his breast pierced by the thorn of the sung rose
you redden with your blood. Assiduously
in the black evening I contrive this poem,
nightingale of the sands and all the seas,
that in exultation, memory and fable,
you burn with love and die in liquid song.

Soy

Soy él que sabe que no es menos vano
que el vano observador que en el espejo
de silencio y cristal sigue el reflejo
o el cuerpo (da lo mismo) del hermano.
Soy, tácitos amigos, él que sabe
que no hay otra venganza que el olvido
ni otro perdón. Un dios ha concedido
al odio humano esta curiosa llave.
Soy él que pese a tan ilustres modos
de errar, no ha descifrado el laberinto
singular y plural, arduo y distinto,
del tiempo, que es de uno y es de todos.
Soy él que es nadie, él que no fue una espada
en la guerra. Soy eco, olvido, nada.

I am

I am he who knows himself no less vain
than the vain looker-on who in the mirror
of glass and silence follows the reflection
or body (it's the same thing) of his brother.
I am, my silent friends, the one who knows
there is no other pardon or revenge
than sheer oblivion. A god has granted
this odd solution to all human hates.
Despite my many wondrous wanderings,
I am the one who never has unravelled
the labyrinth of time, singular, plural,
gruelling, strange, one's own and everyone's.
I am no one. I did not wield a sword
in battle. I am echo, emptiness, nothing.

Quince monedas

A Alicia Jurado

Un poeta oriental

Durante cien otoños he mirado
tu tenue disco.
Durante cien otoños he mirado
tu arco sobre las islas.
Durante cien otoños mis labios
no han sido menos silenciosos.

El desierto

El espacio sin tiempo.
La luna es del color de la arena.
Ahora, precisamente ahora,
mueren los hombres del Metauro y de Trafalgar.

Llueve

¿En qué ayer, en qué patios de Cartago,
cae también esta lluvia?

Asterión

El año me tributa mi pasto de hombres
y en la cisterna hay agua.
En mí se anudan los caminos de piedra.
¿De qué puedo quejarme?
En los atardeceres
me pesa un poco la cabeza de toro.

Fifteen coins

To Alicia Jurado

An Oriental poet

A hundred autumns I have looked upon
your uncertain disk.
A hundred autumns I have looked upon
your rainbow over the islands.
A hundred autumns and my lips
have never been less silent.

The desert

Space without time.
The moon is the same colour as the sand.
Now, at this precise hour,
the men of Metaurus and Trafalgar die.

It is raining

In what yesterday, in what patios of Carthage,
does this rain also fall?

Asterion

The year awards to me my human fodder
and in the cisterns there is water.
In me, the stony paths crisscross.
What can I complain of?
In the late afternoons,
the bull's head weighs on me a little.

Un poeta menor

La meta es el olvido.
Yo he llegado antes.

Génesis iv, 8

Fue en el primer desierto.
Dos brazos arrojaron una gran piedra.
No hubo un grito. Hubo sangre.
Hubo por vez primera la muerte.
Ya no recuerdo si fui Abel o Caín.

Nortumbria, A.D. 900

Que antes del alba lo despojen los lobos;
la espada es el camino más corto.

Miguel de Cervantes

Crueles estrellas y propicias estrellas
presidieron la noche de mi génesis;
debo a las últimas la cárcel
en que soñé Quijote.

El oeste

El callejón final con su poniente.
Inauguración de la pampa.
Inauguración de la muerte.

Estancia El Retiro

El tiempo juega un ajedrez sin piezas
en el patio. El crujido de una rama
rasga la noche. Fuera la llanura

A minor poet

The goal is oblivion.
I have arrived early.

Genesis iv, 8

It was in the original desert.
Two arms let loose a great stone.
There was no cry. There was blood.
For the first time there was death.
I do not recall now if I was Abel or Cain.

Northumbria, A.D. 900

Let the wolves savage him before dawn;
the sword is the quickest way.

Miguel de Cervantes

Both cruel stars and propitious stars
watched over the evening of my genesis;
to the last of those I owe the prison
in which I dreamed of Don Quixote.

The West

The final alley with its setting sun.
Beginning of the pampa.
Beginning of death.

The Retiro Ranch

Time plays a game of chess without the pieces
in the patio. The creaking of a branch
gnaws away at the night. Outside, the plain

leguas de polvo y sueño desparrama.
Sombras los dos, copiamos lo que dictan
otras sombras: Heráclito y Guatama.

El prisionero

Una lima.
La primera de las pesadas puertas de hierro.
Algún día seré libre.

Macbeth

Nuestros actos prosiguen su camino,
que no conoce término.
Maté a mi rey para que Shakespeare
urdiera su tragedia.

Eternidades

La serpiente que ciñe el mar y es el mar,
el repetido remo de Jasón, la joven espada de Sigurd.
Sólo perduran en el tiempo las cosas
que no fueron del tiempo.

Edgar Allen Poe

Los sueños que he soñado. El pozo y el péndulo.
El hombre de las multitudes. Ligeia . . .
Pero también este otro.

El espía

En la pública luz de las batallas
otros dan su vida la patria
Y los recuerda el mármol.
Yo he errado oscuro por ciudades que odio.

squanders its endless leagues of dust and dream.
Both of us shadows, we copy out the dictates
of other shadows: Guatama, Heraclitus.

The prisoner

A file.
The first of the solid iron doors.
One day I will be free.

Macbeth

Our acts continue on their destined way
which does not know an end.
I slew my sovereign so that Shakespeare
might plot his tragedy.

Eternities

The serpent which circles the sea and is the sea,
the recurring oar of Jason, the young sword of Sigurd.
In time, only those things last
which have not been in time.

Edgar Allen Poe

The dreams that I have dreamed. The pit and the pendu-
    lum.
The man of the multitudes. Ligeia . . .
But also this other one.

The spy

In the public glare of battles
others give their lives for their country
and are remembered in marble.
I gave it other things.

Le di otras cosas.
Abjuré de mi honor,
traicioné a quienes me creyeron su amigo,
compré conciencias,
abominé del nombre de la patria,
me resigné a la infamia.

I foreswore my honour,
I betrayed those who believed me their friend,
I purchased consciences,
I abominated the name of my country,
I gave myself up to infamy.

Proteo

Antes que los remeros de Odiseo
fatigaran el mar color de vino
las inasibles formas adivino
de aquel dios cuyo nombre fue Proteo.
Pastor de los rebaños de los mares
y poseedor del don de profecía,
prefería ocultar lo que sabía
y entretejer oráculos dispares.
Urgido por las gentes asumía
la forma de un león o de una hoguera
o de árbol que da sombra a la ribera
o de agua que en el agua se perdía.
De Proteo el egipcio no te asombres,
tú, que eres uno y eres muchos hombres.

Proteus

Before the oarsmen of Odysseus
were able to exhaust the wine-dark sea,
I can divine the indefinable forms
of that old god whose name was Proteus.
Shepherd of the wave-flocks of the waters
and wielder of the gift of prophecy,
he liked to make a secret of his knowledge
and weave a pattern of ambiguous answers.
At the demand of people, he took on
the substance of a lion or a bonfire
or a tree, spreading shade on the river bank
or water which would disappear in water.
Do not take fright at Proteus the Egyptian,
you, who are one, and also many men.

Brunanburh, A.D. 937

Nadie a tu lado.
Anoche maté a un hombre en la batalla.
Era animoso y alto, de la clara estirpe de Anlaf.
La espada entró en el pecho, un poco a la izquierda.
Rodó por tierra y fue una cosa,
una cosa del cuervo.
En vano lo esperarás, mujer que no he visto.
No lo traerán las naves que huyéron
sobre el agua amarilla.
En la hora del alba,
tu mano desde el sueño lo buscará.
Tu lecho está frío.
Anoche maté a un hombre en Brunanburh.

No one at your side.
Last night I did a man to death in battle.
He was spirited and tall, of the clear line of Anlaf.
The sword went into his breast, a shade to the left.
He turned on the ground and was a thing,
an object for crows.
In vain will you await him, wife I have not seen.
They will not bear him back, the ships that fled
over the yellow waters.
In the hour of the dawn,
out of a dream, your hand will reach for him.
Your couch is cold.
Last night I killed a man in Brunanburh.

El ciego

Lo han despojado del diverso mundo,
de los rostros, que son lo que eran antes,
de las cercanas calles, hoy distantes,
y del cóncavo azul, ayer profundo.
De los libros le queda lo que deja
la memoria, esa forma del olvido
que retiene el formato, no el sentido,
y que los meros títulos refleja.
El desnivel acecha. Cada paso
puede ser la caída. Soy el lento
prisionero de un tiempo soñoliento
que no marca su aurora ni su ocaso.
Es de noche. No hay otros. Con el verso
debo labrar mi insípido universo.

II

Desde mi nacimiento, que fue el noventa y nueve
de la cóncava parra y el aljibe profundo,
el tiempo minucioso, que en la memoria es breve,
me fue hurtando las formas visibles de este mundo.
Los días y las noches limaron los perfiles
de las letras humanas y los rostros amados;
en vano interrogaron mis ojos agotados
las vanas bibliotecas y los vanos atriles.
El azul y el bermejo son ahora una niebla
y dos voces inútiles. El espejo que miro
es una cosa gris. En el jardín aspiro,
amigos, una lóbrega rosa de la tiniebla.
Ahora sólo perduran las formas amarillas
y sólo puedo ver para ver pesadillas.

The blind man

I

He is divested of the diverse world,
of faces, which still stay as once they were,
of the adjoining streets, now far away,
and of the concave sky, once infinite.
Of books, he keeps no more than what is left him
by memory, that brother of forgetting,
which keeps the formula but not the feeling
and which reflects no more than tag and name.
Traps lie in wait for me. My every step
might be a fall. I am a prisoner
shuffling through a time which feels like dream,
taking no note of mornings or of sunsets.
It is night. I am alone. In verse like this,
I must create my insipid universe.

II

Since I was born, in 1899,
beside the concave vine and the deep cistern,
frittering time, so brief in memory,
kept taking from me all my eye-shaped world.
Both days and nights would wear away the profiles
of human letters and of well-loved faces.
My wasted eyes would ask their useless questions
of pointless libraries and lecterns.
Blue and vermilion both are now a fog,
both useless sounds. The mirror I look into
is grey. I breathe a rose across the garden,
a wistful rose, my friends, out of the twilight.
Only the shades of yellow stay with me
and I can see only to look on nightmares.

Un ciego

No sé cuál es la cara que me mira
cuando miro la cara del espejo;
no sé qué anciano acecha en su reflejo
con silenciosa y ya cansada ira.
Lento en mi sombra, con la mano exploro
mis invisibles rasgos. Un destello
me alcanza. He vislumbrado tu cabello
que es de ceniza o es aún de oro.
Repito que he perdido solamente
la vana superficie de las cosas.
El consuelo es de Milton y es valiente,
pero pienso en las letras y en las rosas.
Pienso que si pudiera ver mi cara
sabría quién soy en esta tarde rara.

A blind man

I do not know what face is looking back
whenever I look at the face in the mirror;
I do not know what old face seeks its image
in silent and already weary anger.
Slow in my blindness, with my hand I feel
the contours of my face. A flash of light
gets through to me. I have made out your hair,
colour of ash and at the same time, gold.
I say again that I have lost no more
than the inconsequential skin of things.
These wise words come from Milton, and are noble,
but then I think of letters and of roses.
I think, too, that if I could see my features,
I would know who I am, this precious afternoon.

Temí que el porvenir (que ya declina)
sería un profundo corredor de espejos
indistintos, ociosos y menguantes,
una repetición de vanidades,
y en la penumbra que precede al sueño
rogué a mis dioses, cuyo nombre ignoro,
que enviaran algo o alguien a mis días.
Lo hicieron. Es la Patria. Mis mayores
la sirvieron con largas proscripciones,
con penurias, con hambre, con batallas,
aquí de nuevo está el hermoso riesgo.
No soy aquellas sombras tutelares
que honré con versos que no olvida el tiempo.
Estoy ciego. He cumplido los setenta;
no soy el oriental Francisco Borges
que murió con dos balas en el pecho,
entre las agonías de los hombres,
en el hedor de un hospital de sangre,
pero la Patria, hoy profanada quiere
que con mi oscura pluma de gramático,
docta en las nimiedades académicas
y ajena a los trabajos de la espada,
congregue el gran rumor de la epopeya
y exija mi lugar. Lo estoy haciendo.

I feared that the future, now already dwindling,
would be an extending corridor of mirrors,
useless and vague, their images on the wane,
a repetition of all vanities,
and in the half-light which precedes the dream,
I begged my gods, whose names I do not know,
to send something or someone into my days.
They did. It is my country. My own forebears
gave themselves up to it through long proscriptions,
in penury, in hunger, and in battle.
Here, once again, comes the alluring challenge.
I am not with those tutelary figures
I praised in verses still alive in time.
I am blind, and I have lived out seventy years.
I am not Francisco Borges from the east
who died with a brace of bullets in his breast
among the final agonies of men
in the death-stench of a hospital of blood;
but my country, violated now, insists
that with my tentative grammarian's pen,
well-schooled in academic tinkerings,
far from the warlike business of the sword,
I assemble the great rumble of the epic
and carve out my own place. I am doing it.

Elegía

Tres muy antiguas caras me desvelan:
una el Océano, que habló con Claudio,
otra el Norte de aceros ignorantes
y atroces en la aurora y el ocaso,
la tercera la muerte, ese otro nombre
del incesante tiempo que nos roe.
La carga secular de los ayeres
de la historia que fue o que fue soñada
me abruma, personal como una culpa.
Pienso en la nave ufana que devuelve
a los mares el cuerpo de Scyld Sceaving
que reinó en Dinamarca bajo el cielo;
pienso en el alto lobo, cuyas riendas
eran sierpes, que dio al barco incendiado
la blancura del dios hermoso y muerto;
pienso en piratas cuya carne humana
es dispersión y limo bajo el peso
de los mares que fueron su aventura;
pienso en las tumbas que los navegantes
vieron desde boreales Odiseas.
Pienso en mi propria, en mi perfecta muerte,
sin la urna cineraria y sin la lágrima.

Elegy

Three very ancient faces stay with me:
one is the Ocean, which would talk with Claudius,
another the North, with its unfeeling temper,
savage both at sunrise and at sunset;
the third is Death, that other name we give
to passing time, which wears us all away.
The secular burden of those yesterdays
from history which happened or was dreamed,
oppresses me as personally as guilt.
I think of the proud ship, carrying back
to sea the body of Scyld Sceaving,
who ruled in Denmark underneath the sky;
I think of the great wolf, whose reins were serpents,
who lent the burning boat the purity
and whiteness of the beautiful dead god;
I think of pirates too, whose human flesh
is scattered through the slime beneath the weight
of waters which were ground for their adventures;
I think of mausoleums which the sailors
saw in the course of Northern odyssies.
I think of my own death, my perfect death,
without a funeral urn, without a tear.

El desterrado (1977)

Alguien recorre los senderos de Itaca
y no se acuerda de su rey, que fue a Troya
hace ya tantos años;
alguien piensa en las tierras heredadas
y en el arado nuevo y el hijo
y es acaso feliz.
En el confín del orbe yo, Ulises,
descendí a la Casa de Hades
y vi la sombra del tebano Tiresias
que desligó el amor de las serpientes
y la sombra de Heracles
que mata sombras de leones en la pradera
y asimismo está en el Olimpo.
Alguien hoy anda por Bolívar y Chile
y puede ser feliz o no serlo.
Quién me diera ser él.

The exile (1977)

Someone makes tracks along the paths of Ithaca
and has forgotten his king, who was at Troy
so many years ago;
someone is thinking of his new-won lands,
his new plough and his son,
and is happy, in the main.
Within the confines of the globe, myself, Ulysses,
descended deep into the Hall of Hades
and saw the shade of Tiresius of Thebes
who unlocked the love of the serpents
and the shade of Hercules
who kills the shades of lions on the plain
and at the same time occupies Olympus.
Someone today walks streets – Chile, Bolívar –
perhaps happy, perhaps not.
I wish I could be he.

En memoria de Angelica

¡Cuántas posibles vidas se habrán ido
en esta pobre y diminuta muerte,
cuántas posibles vidas que la suerte
daría a la memoria o al olvido!
Cuanda yo muera morirá un pasado;
con esta flor un porvenir ha muerto
en las aguas que ignoran, un abierto
porvenir por los astros arrasado.
Yo, como ella, muero de infinitos
destinos que el azar no me depara;
busca mi sombra los gastados mitos
de una patria que siempre dio la cara.
Un breve mármol cuida su memoria;
sobre nosotros crece, atroz, la historia.

In memory of Angelica

How many possible lives must have gone out
in this so modest and diminutive death,
how many possible lives, which fate would turn
to memory, or else oblivion?
When I die too, a certain past will die;
with this small bloom, a yet-to-be has died
in the unfeeling water, a white future
blindly obliterated by the stars.
Like her, I am dead to infinite destinies
which chance makes inaccessible to me.
My shadow seeks out all the lifeless myths
within my country, which was always brave.
A slab of marble tends her memory.
Over us looms atrocious history.

Mis libros

Mis libros (que no saben que yo existo)
son tan parte de mí como este rostro
de sienes grises y de grises ojos
que vanamente busco en los cristales
y que recorro con la mano cóncava.
No sin alguna lógica amargura
pienso que las palabras esenciales
que me expresan están en esas hojas
que no saben quién soy, no en las que he escrito.
Mejor así. Las voces de los muertos
me dirán para siempre.

My books

My books (which do not know that I exist)
are as much part of me as is this face,
the temples gone to grey and the eyes grey,
the face I vainly look for in the mirror,
tracing its outline with a concave hand.
Not without understandable bitterness,
I feel now that the quintessential words
expressing me are in those very pages
which do not know me, not in those I have written.
It is better so. The voices of the dead
will speak to me for ever.

Talismanes

Un ejemplar de la primera edición de la *Edda Islandorum*
de Snorri, impresa en Dinamarca.
Los cinco tomos de la obra de Schopenhauer.
Los dos tomos de las *Odiseas* de Chapman.
Una espada que guerreó – el desierto.
Un mate con un pie de serpientes que mi bisabuelo trajo
de Lima.
Un prisma de cristal.
Unos daguerrotipos borrosos.
Un globo terráqueo de madera que me dio Cecilia Inge-
nieros y que fue de su padre.
Un bastón de puño encorvado que anduvo por las llanuras
de América, por Colombia y por Texas.
Varios cilindros de metal con diplomas.
La toga y el birrete de un doctorado.
Las Empresas de Saavedra Fajardo, en olorosa pasta es-
pañola.
La memoria de una mañana.
Líneas de Virgilio y de Frost.
La voz de Macedonio Fernández.
El amor o el diálogo de unos pocos.
Ciertamente son talismanes, pero de nada sirven contra la
sombra que no puedo nombrar, contra la sombra que no
debo nombrar.

Talismans

A copy of the first edition of the *Edda Islandorum*, by
  Snorri, printed in Denmark.
The five volumes of the work of Schopenhauer.
The two volumes of Chapman's *Odyssey*.
A sword which fought in the desert.
A maté gourd with serpent feet which my great-grand-
  father brought from Lima.
A crystal prism.
A few eroded daguerrotypes.
A terraqueous wooden globe which Cecilia Ingenieros gave
  me and which belonged to her father.
A stick with a curved handle with which I walked on the
  plains of America, in Colombia and in Texas.
Various metal cylinders with diplomas.
The gown and mortarboard of a doctorate.
Las Empresas, by Saavedra Fajardo, bound in good-smell-
  ing Spanish board.
The memory of a morning.
Lines of Virgil and Frost.
The voice of Macedonio Fernandez.
The love or the conversation of a few people.
Certainly they are talismans, but useless against the dark
  I cannot name, the dark I must not name.

La cierva blanca

¿De qué agreste balada de la verde Inglaterra,
de qué lámina persa, de qué región arcana
de las noches y días que nuestro ayer encierra,
vino la cierva blanca que soñé esta mañana?
Duraría un segundo. La vi cruzar el prado
y perderse en el oro de una tarde ilusoria,
leve criatura hecha de un poco de memoria
y de un poco de olvido, cierva de un solo lado.
Los númenes que rigen este curioso mundo
me dejaron soñarte pero no ser tu dueño;
tal vez en un recodo del porvenir profundo
te encontraré de nuevo, cierva blanca de un sueño.
Yo también soy un sueño fugitivo que dura
unos días más que el sueño del prado y la blancura.

The white deer

Out of what country ballad of green England,
or Persian etching, out of what secret region
of nights and days enclosed in our lost past
came the white deer I dreamed of in the dawn?
A moment's flash. I saw it cross the meadow
and vanish in the golden afternoon,
a lithe, illusory creature, half-remembered
and half-imagined, deer with a single side.
The presences which rule this curious world
have let me dream of you but not command you.
Perhaps in a recess of the unplumbed future,
again I will find you, white deer from my dream.
I too am dream, lasting a few days longer
than that bright dream of whiteness and green fields.

La rosa profunda
A Susana Bombal

A los quinientos años de la Héjira
Persia miró desde sus alminares
la invasión de las lanzas del desierto
y Attar de Nishapur miró una rosa
y le dijo con tácita palabra
como él que piensa, no como él que reza:
– Tu vaga esfera está en mi mano. El tiempo
Nos encorva a los dos y nos ignora
en esta tarde de un jardín perdido.
Tu leve peso es húmedo en el aire.
La incesante pleamar de tu fragancia
sube a mi vieja cara que declina
pero te sé más lejos que aquel niño
que te entrevió en las láminas de un sueño
o aquí en este jardín, una mañana.
La blancura del sol puede ser tuya
o el oro de la luna o la bermeja
firmeza de la espada en la victoria.
Soy ciego y nada sé, pero preveo
que son más los caminos. Cada cosa
es infinitas cosas. Eres música,
firmamentos, palacios, ríos, ángeles,
rosa profunda, ilimitada, íntima,
que el Señor mostrará a mis ojos muertos.

The unending rose

To Susana Bombal

Five hundred years in the wake of the Hegira,
Persia looked down from its minarets
on the invasion of the desert lances,
and Attar of Nishapur gazed on a rose,
addressing it in words which had no sound,
as one who thinks rather than one who prays:
'Your fragile globe is in my hand; and time
is bending both of us, both unaware,
this afternoon, in a forgotten garden.
Your brittle shape is humid in the air.
The steady, tidal fullness of your fragrance
rises up to my old, declining face.
But I know you far longer than that child
who glimpsed you in the layers of a dream
or here, in this garden, once upon a morning.
The whiteness of the sun may well be yours
or the moon's gold, or else the crimson stain
on the hard sword-edge in the victory.
I am blind and I know nothing, but I see
there are more ways to go; and everything
is an infinity of things. You, you are music,
rivers, firmaments, palaces and angels,
O endless rose, intimate, without limit,
which the Lord will finally show to my dead eyes.'

Notes

'Tankas'. I have attempted to adapt to our prosody the Japanese form that consists of a first line of five syllables, then one of seven, one of five, and the last two of seven. Who knows how these exercises sound to an Oriental ear. The original form also ignores rhyme.

'The gold of the tigers'. For the ring of nine nights, the curious reader can look up chapter 49 of the Lesser Edda. The name of the ring was Draupnir.

'In memory of Angelica'. Borges' niece was drowned in a swimming pool at the age of six.